MW01234465

The Book of Daniel:
Hellbound and Down

Thanks for reading!

Lee P---

The Book of Daniel: Hellbound and Down

Lee Pierce

Copyright © 2007, 2014, 2022 by Lee Pierce

All rights reserved. This book or any portion thereof may not be reproduced or used in any manner whatsoever without the express written permission of the publisher except for the use of brief quotations in a book review or scholarly journal.

First Printing: 2014

Introduction

Quite a few people are going to be disappointed, or even upset, with this book. It's the first book in a trilogy, and that's going to make some people angry. Let me explain: when I say trilogy, I mean an actual trilogy. Three books, each with their own central plot, that make up one longer story. With that in mind, I'm going to go ahead and spoil the ending for you: the end of this book does not end the story. Like I said, some people will get angry about that. It's not like how so many movies or books are created today, with a story that, if it does well, will have sequels added on. This is more like *Lord of the Rings*. When this book ends, there will still be many dangling plots and untold stories.

So, please, be patient. Just because the book is done, doesn't mean the story is over.

1

In which we meet our hero and his strange sidekick, take a tour around the city and learn of its history, and receive odd visitors and cryptic warnings.

He ran his hands through his hair as the smoke curled off his jacket in lazy spirals, making sure his hair wasn't on fire. Trips like this were always tough. They were like being born as a full-grown man.

The imp wandered into the room and put on a fake shocked expression at the sight of him, before walking over and holding the tip of a cigar against him.

"What are you doing?" he asked the imp, the fatigue in his voice apparent even to him.

"Just checking." The imp started to go over to the nearest chair in the office, but stopped and turned back to him. "You don't mind, do you?"

"Bring it here," he said. The imp walked to him again and leaned in. The man snapped his fingers and a small flame erupted, lighting the cigar. The imp smiled and inhaled deeply.

"Knew you were good for something." He resumed his trip to the chair and the man watched with weary amusement as the imp tried to haul himself into the rolling office chair. With nothing else in the room, the chair rolled with the imp half on it, until it finally stopped with a thud against the nearest wall.

Once the imp looked like he was finally seated comfortably, he took the man in slowly.

"So, Danny, nice trip?" the imp asked, a mischievous grin spreading on his face, making him look slightly evil, and completely insane.

"The same as always," Danny replied. He let out a sigh and started to lean back, stopping only when the imp started waving his hands and almost jumped out of the chair.

"Whoa there, brother," the little man exclaimed, still flapping about excitedly. "Don't lean back. Don't want you ruining the furniture anymore than you already have."

"What do you mean? My back hurts."

"There's still some smoke coming off you. I just tried to light a cigar on you. Chances are, you're still a bit warm. Are you that exhausted?"

Danny simply nodded, and leaned forward once more. He let his head fall so that he was staring straight at the floor, his bangs falling into his eyes. Badly need a haircut, he thought. Have to remember that when there's more time.

The imp sat in his chair, smoking, and sizing Danny up. Finally, with all the casualness of a baby elephant, he asked, "Did you find it?"

Danny shook his head.

"Ever think about giving up?"

Danny pondered this for a moment. Yes, he thought about it every day. But he would never say that out loud. Instead, he simply said, "I can't give up."

"Obviously." The imp dropped down out of

the chair and stubbed his cigar out on the floor. He walked into the adjoining room, calling back over his shoulder, "Water?"

"Yeah."

He could hear the imp in the next room, searching for something clean to put water in. Danny took the moment to check his pockets, making sure everything was still there. The pouch in his left breast pocket was missing. He'd have to replace that before he tried again. He checked the locket around his neck, feeling the safety in its weight. It was still there, that was the important thing.

The imp returned bearing a chipped coffee cup. Danny accepted it gratefully and emptied it in one gulp.

"More?" the imp asked.

Danny shook his head, letting the coolness of the water work its way down his throat. "How long have I been gone?" he finally asked.

"Three days," the imp answered.

A dark expression crossed Danny's face before he nodded. He was wasting time. He stood up and started to exit the room. The imp stopped him.

"Look, Danny-boy, I'm a bit worried about you."

"I'm fine," was his only reply.

"You certainly don't look fine. I think it's time to start re-thinking our priorities here."

"Loki," Danny said. He stared deep into the imp's eyes, and the imp was transfixed, as always, with the flames that danced in Danny's eyes after one of his trips. "I have to go on. This needs to be done."

Loki shook his head, trying to clear his mind. "Okay," he finally said. "But why you? Maybe we could find somebody else do it for a little while?"

"There isn't anybody else," Danny said quietly. He stepped past the imp and headed to the bathroom. He needed a shower badly. "Who else would do it? I'm fairly sure you and I are some of the few people that actually know about all this."

"Danny," Loki called after him. "You can't keep doing this to yourself. Taking constant trips into Hell can't be good for you."

Danny stopped and smiled. No, trips into Hell probably weren't good for anybody. But if Danny was successful, it could potentially save the world. And with that thought in his mind, Danny went to get his shower.

He let the clothes lazily fall off his body, feeling his core temperature dropping with every passing moment. It was the one thing he hated about the trips, but feeling like your insides are cooking was just part of the job.

The water stung at his face as Danny stepped into the shower, letting the water slowly wash over him, feeling the dirt and grime, the sulfur and brimstone, fall away. He had no idea how long he stood like this, lost in thought, the water cascading onto his head and pushing his hair into his face, only that when he came to the bathroom was filled with steam. He greatly disliked this feeling, that time was slipping away, time that was so precious to his mission. But he had things he needed to tend to, and his own well-being was one of those. Besides, time was always a bit of an illusion to him anyway. His sense of urgency had less to do with any actual hurry, and more to do with the fact that he felt he was so close to finishing with the whole damn mess.

He threw back the shower curtain and was immediately struck by the image in the mirror. It was down in the bottom corner, blurred by the condensation, but still clear enough to see the features on the woman's face, the fiery red hair, to notice the blood flowing from her nose and lips, to see the anguished look in her eyes.

The one thing he wasn't, though, was scared. He had seen too many visions over the course of his life to let one frighten him anymore. This was just another. Maybe a spirit, maybe a vision of the future, he didn't know. There wasn't an exact science to these things. But he was transfixed by the woman. She was beautiful, and sad, and defiant, all at the same time. Danny thought perhaps a ghost based on the haunted look she had. Whatever she was, he had a sudden, overwhelming, urge to help her.

It was this thought that made him paranoid. Maybe he was meant to see this, maybe it was purposely sent to him. Maybe it was just a way to distract him from the matters at hand. If it was, he was in trouble. It meant that his enemies could now get to him, could influence his decisions. He touched the locket that hung around his neck, feeling its eternal coolness in his fingers, and wondered if he was in more danger than he was aware of.

He stepped out of the shower and approached the mirror, but the image grew no clearer. Knowing what would happen, but doing it anyway, he reached out and tried to wipe the fog away, causing the image to disappear as well. It didn't matter. He had learned everything he could from it.

He walked into the kitchen to find Loki shuffling jars around, gauging their contents and writing in a notepad. Without looking at him, Loki said, "You're gonna need to restock."

"I just saw a woman."

Loki turned to look at him. "Where?"

"In the bathroom," Danny answered.

"Oh," was the reply, followed by a laugh. "I do that all the time. I just have the decency not to tell you about it."

"What?" Danny asked, distracted, before finally catching the imp's meaning. "Oh, no, not like that. It was, like, a vision."

"*Like* a vision, or an actual vision?"

"An actual vision." Danny sat on the stool nearest him, still lost in thought. "She was beautiful."

"Yeah, my visions always are too."

"I don't know anything about it though," Danny sighed. "No who, where, when, or why."

"Well then, it's best just to put it out of mind, isn't it?" Loki walked to Danny and patted his leg sympathetically. "You should get some rest before you go again. Let yourself recharge a little."

Danny nodded. "I will. But I want to get those supplies first."

"That's fine. I've got some errands to run

anyway."

Danny had been to all of the greatest cities on Earth, but in his opinion, none of them could touch Austin, TX. Maybe there were bodies of water more beautiful than Lake Travis, and maybe there were peaks more spectacular than Mount Bonnell, but that didn't matter. The city had a vibe to it unlike any other place he'd ever lived. It reminded him of ancient Rome.

Without the gladiator fights, of course.

They got into his beat up old Camaro convertible and drove down South Congress, Danny enjoying the sunshine against his face. It was a beautiful May day, and his mind was starting to clear.

"Supplies first?" he asked Loki.

"Actually, if you don't mind, I'd like to run my errand first," the little man replied.

Loki pointed at an empty lot across the street from Guero's, and Danny parked. There was little conversation as they started up the street, Danny lost in thought, Loki consumed by whatever images ran through his head. Danny almost ran him over though when Loki came to a stop in front of Joe's Coffee. The imp approached the window, which was unusually empty for this time of day, and stood waiting. No one noticed him.

"Hey," he said. "Hey! Excuse me!"

The guy behind the counter looked at Danny. Danny pointed down, where the man could just see the top of Loki's head.

"Can I help you?" the barista asked Loki, slightly confused.

Loki laid a ten on the counter. "Two Iced Turbos. Keep the change." With that, he waddled around to the other side of the shack to await his order.

When the drinks were ready, Loki scooped them up and walked over to the nearest table, where an abandoned issue of the *Austin Chronicle* lay. He sat down and began to read.

"This is your errand?" Danny asked, sipping the coffee.

"Yes. It's my errand for you. You need coffee for the energy. You need to sit in the sun and look at the pretty girls walking down the street to clear your head. These trips make you a bit loopy."

Danny had to smile at that. For as annoying and useless as Loki could be most of the time, he was always very perceptive about certain things.

Danny sat back and closed his eyes, exhaling deeply. The caffeine *was* feeling good in his system. The slight breeze felt good in his hair. He slowly let himself come back down, letting everything he had seen and felt the last three days leave his body like a poison. He supposed that might just be what it was. Hell was a bad place, so it shouldn't come as a surprise that spending any amount of time there would make a person feel bad.

After what seemed like an eternity, he felt Loki tug on his arm.

"We've got company," he said.

Danny opened his eyes and saw few people. It was a Thursday, and most people were still at work. The people out and about seemed to be mostly tourists. Behind him, a conversation buzzed between two writers about the merits of one's new screenplay. He looked to his left, towards downtown, and he saw them.

Two humanoid figures were walking up the street, their long black hair flowing behind them. They wore matching long leather dusters, complementing their black wardrobe. They both wore expressions that they were not to be bothered. And they both had their eyes locked on Danny.

"You got the locket?" Loki asked.

"Yeah, but I'm not worried about these two." Danny looked at Loki and grinned reassuringly. "They're not here to fight. Besides, I'm not sure if the locket would stop them anyway."

They came to a stop at the table.

"Daniel," the taller of the two said.

"Hello, Michael," Danny said. He looked at the other. "Augustyne."

The smaller one nodded.

"Do you mind if we join you?" Michael asked.

"Of course not," Danny said, trying to keep his tone jovial.

Loki quickly piped up. "Well, I mind. I mind tremendously."

"I do not believe anyone asked you, imp," Michael answered in a bored tone. The two seated themselves opposite Danny and Loki.

"So," Danny asked, "are you two just out for a stroll, or is this a business matter?"

The two exchanged glances. "We have a message for you," Augustyne said.

"You need to stop immediately," Michael told

him.

Danny understood right away.

"I would think you would be on my side on this," he said, acting stunned at the news.

"You know better," Michael said. "You are making both sides look bad, and, frankly, it is angering some." They paused, giving Danny a deep, dark look.

"So, if I stop, are you going to take care of everything?" Danny asked.

Augustyne looked at Michael with a strange expression. "We have not been given the order. You know we cannot act unless we are told to in this sort of situation."

"This situation is a huge threat. Why hasn't an order been given? I mean, if I'm really doing such a bad job, I would think you would want to take care of it," Danny asked.

"It does not matter why we do what we do," Michael barked. "We do not need to justify ourselves to you."

"Sorry, I'm just curious. I'm assuming this is being treated as a huge threat, isn't it?"

"Back off, Daniel. That is all you need to know." With that, Michael got up and stalked away. Augustyne trailed behind for a moment, gave Danny a pained expression, and then followed. At his side, Loki sighed.

"This is what I hate about angels. Always so cryptic. And very anti-social."

Danny watched the two walk away while Loki went back to his paper. He kept a watch on the street even as the two angels disappeared over the horizon, looking out for anyone else that might be coming to see him. There was no one. And with that, Danny knew he was alone in this mission.

After a moment, he felt Loki's eyes back on him.

"What?" he asked.

"I was just wondering..." Loki paused. "Are you sure we should be doing this after all? I mean, they seemed pretty adamant about stopping."

Danny nodded. "I've thought about that. I've thought about it for a long, long time. And after all that time, I came to the conclusion that, yes, this should be done. God would want it done."

"Oh," Loki laughed. "And now you presume to know what God wants?"

"Well, I'd like to think I know Him well enough to say that."

"Well, let's hope so. For your sake." Loki folded the paper and set it back on the table. "Shall we go then? Or would you rather wait for some more old friends of the heavenly persuasion?"

"No, let's go. I've had enough surprises for one day."

The pair walked down Congress until they reached the bridge that crossed the river and connected downtown to South Austin. They descended the stairs to the walkway that ran along the lower side, but instead of walking across, they continued down until they reached the ground.

From here, they could see the underside of the bridge looming some seventy-five feet above them. Thousands of bats clung to the bridge, sleeping the day away. Danny always wondered why they had chosen this spot, and why the people of the city had chosen to hold an annual festival to celebrate their famous "Bat Bridge". He had always suspected it had something to do with what was hidden in the base of the bridge.

The design and construction of the bridge had been overseen by a man, originally from Romania, by the name of Alexander Stusevyant. Stusevyant had come from his country to the States carrying more than just his knowledge of architecture. He also brought his extensive knowledge of the occult.

It had long been rumored that during the construction, Stusevyant was trying to avoid a pair of particularly nasty underworld beings. The kind with horns and sharp teeth. In order to find a place to hide, he had designed the lower half of the bridge to be a conductor of magical energy, a focal point for all of the American southwest. That energy had left the walls of reality very thin at the bridge's base, and with a few simple spells, he was able to create a portal back to a safe house. Unfortunately, due to the complicated magic needed to create the bridge, and his exhaustion from constantly fighting off his pursuers, he died shortly after construction.

But the bridge, and its energies, held.

Danny and Loki walked into the shadows, past the homeless man fishing the river, and into a world of graffiti and garbage. It was the perfect place to hide a shop dealing in the less desirables.

Under a giant white spray painted 9, Loki

paused. "Here," he said. Danny knocked three times, and a door appeared. He pushed it open. Behind the door was a place that most humans could never imagine.

A quick glance would've revealed a street bazaar, but upon closer inspection, you would have realized that no bazaar in the world sold items like this. Every shop along the street seemed to specialize in mystical items or pseudo-religious trinkets. The area was a tribute to medieval times.

Ancient brownstones dominated either side of the street, running for two blocks and ending in a cul de sac. Tents lined the sidewalk, selling cheaply made wares, ran by shady looking salesmen. Smoke rose out of fires and large iron cauldrons. The cul de sac itself was virtually empty, with the exception of a giant fountain with a crudely carved marble bust of an extremely obese man in the center.

The rumor went that after Stusevyant died, the area he had used as his retreat sat empty for decades. At some later point in time, an American businessman, drunk and lost, stumbled upon it accidentally, apparently having dabbled a bit in magic and making him able to enter. Realizing he had a location that would be his for free, he set about creating a set of doors to the area across the world, building a global market for the sale of magical items. He topped it off by creating a shrine to himself, the most unflattering monument that had ever been seen. After making millions off of his project, he died, leaving the marketplace in disarray.

This was the scene Danny and Loki were confronted with as they walked down the cracked asphalt. Danny had never been a fan of this place, but it was convenient, having a door in Austin. And he had built a rapport with a shop keeper, one of the few decent ones in this place.

Danny noted that many of the shops now seemed closed, their shutters pulled, dust collecting on the windows. That suited him just fine. They only needed to make one stop anyway.

Zedediah's shop was the last before the cul de sac. It too looked like it had went out of business, but Danny pushed the door open nonetheless. It only stuck for a moment.

"The place looks deserted," Loki said as they walked in, careful not to disturb any of the vast quantities of dirt that had accumulated.

"It's not." Danny called out, "Come out! There's nothing to be afraid of!"

"Danny? Is that you?" came the reply.

Danny called back, "Of course it's me. Who else would come here?"

Part of the paneling from behind the counter slid open and out waddled Zedediah. Danny guessed he had once been human, but he wasn't even close these days. It looked as if someone had stapled multiple body parts to him and turned his skin an iridescent shade of blue. As he walked on his three legs, a tail drug uselessly behind him. To become like this, he had to have made some dark wizard very angry back in the day. Danny still liked him, despite the fiendish appearance.

"Want to explain why were you hiding, Zed?"

Danny asked.

"Dark times, old friend." He held out one of his hands and Danny shook it. "What brings you here?"

Loki handed him a list. "Supplies."

Zed looked over the list, nodding as he went. He stopped and looked at the imp with a grin. "I've told you I can't get you this. Creating life isn't something I deal in."

Loki shrugged. "Worth a shot."

"True, little one. And who hasn't wanted to create a woman for himself at one time or another?" Zed went back to looking at the list. "I've got all the rest," he said, as he began moving to racks and shelves around the shop, piling everything into a sack he grabbed from the counter.

"Zed," Danny said, "what do you mean by dark times?"

Zed paused, still looking at the list. "You need remungus powder I see," he said. "Still haven't found the stone then."

"No," Danny answered. "But I'm getting close."

Zed nodded and went about filling the rest of the order. When he was finished, he returned to the counter. He stood before Danny for a moment, as if sizing him up.

"Can I give you a word of advice, Daniel?"

"Sure," Danny said. He was feeling a bit puzzled by all of this.

Zed's face became grave and cold. "Finish it, Danny. Find the stones, and for all that's holy, do it quickly. Or call the damn thing off."

Danny took a moment to choose his words. He finally asked what he felt was connected to this. "Why were you hiding? Was it because of me?"

Loki's eyes went back and forth between the two. Finally, Zed lowered his head.

"Dark times are coming, Danny. Forces are gathering. It's going to get bad. Maybe as bad as it can get. For you," he now raised his eyes and locked onto Danny's, "and for anyone that knows you."

Danny looked a bit panicked. "Is everything okay?" he asked. "Nothing stolen from the shop?"

"No, Danny, nothing stolen. Everything is still completely safe. Just had a little... physical altercation."

A mixture of fear and anger rose in Danny's stomach. "Who did this, Zed? Who's after you?"

Zed waved his hand. "Don't matter. I've said what needs to be said." He slid the bag across the counter to Danny. "Two hundred for the supplies. The advice was free. Use it as you will."

The car ride home was uncomfortable, so Danny dropped Loki back at the apartment, and then took off again. He needed some time to himself. Loki had barely said a word once they left Zed's. He seemed to be lost in his own thoughts. That was just fine with Danny. He had too much on his mind to make conversation.

He drove down First Street for awhile, finally coming to a stop at Freddie's, a little outdoor hamburger joint. He grabbed one of the tables underneath the elm trees, and sat overlooking the little creek that ran behind the restaurant until a waitress came to take his order.

"Bleu cheese burger and a Shiner," he told

her. She nodded and walked away, returning promptly with his drink. He let the cold beer run down his throat, savoring its sweetness. There were a lot of good beers in the world, but nothing could beat a Texas beer.

His food arrived a short time later, and he sat eating, feeling the breeze in his hair and watching the people around him. Quite a few people had brought their dogs with them, some were playing in a ring toss tournament, others were just lazily chatting with friends on a glorious spring day.

Danny's thoughts were preoccupied with today's events.

He had been warned once and questioned twice about backing off. Forces were gathering, and they were going after anyone that associated with him. It was troubling news. Bad enough the angels were taking a non-involvement stance, but if there was someone out there gunning for him, he wanted to know who. There was nothing worse than fighting an enemy that you couldn't see.

Perhaps he should back off. Danny didn't know if he could stand to see someone he knew die. He'd already seen it happen too often before, and thought he had put it all behind him years ago. He'd had a chance to back off before, not long after he started down this path, but Loki had convinced him to carry on. But the stakes were getting higher now. Maybe it was time to walk away, concentrate on other things. Maybe the girl in the mirror.

As a Lonestar sunset cast its rays over him,

Danny made his decision. It was, as usual, the people around him that did it. As they casually enjoyed their evening, Danny wondered what they would do if they knew it was their last night on earth. If he were to just walk away, it very well could be. Collecting the stones was important. It could save the world. And he knew that Loki and his other friends could protect themselves, just as Zed had. Besides, he would hate to give up.

That would make the last two hundred years of his life a bit of a waste.

2

In which Danny tries to have a relaxing evening, but is interrupted by a femme fatale.

The Horseshoe on Llamar was definitely what you'd call a dive bar. But then again, in Austin, basically every bar south of 6th Street was a dive. Just another reason Danny loved this place.

It was nestled closely between two other buildings, in what looked to have once been a half-hearted attempt at a small strip mall. Instead, you were left with three run down stone buildings, the neon sign from one casting the tiny parking lot in a pinkish-red light. The bar itself was everything you'd expect looking at it from the outside: old, dingy green carpet, sagging vinyl bar stools, a pool table in one corner, old-school jukebox opposite it, shuffleboard table across, and the closet-sized rooms that passed for restrooms, if pissing in a trough was your idea of a restroom. Cigarette smoke hung in the air, and even though Austin had banned public smoking years ago, no one complained. The place was just too laid back for that. Like most other places in South Austin, celebrities would stumble in from time to time. Danny once shared a beer with Robert Rodriguez and his nieces, another night he listened to Matthew McConaughey play the jukebox all night. No one bothered them. Everybody was too cool for that.

Behind the bar, a middle-aged woman danced to the sounds of Lynyrd Skynyrd while passing out beers. She was slightly overweight and had a crazy look in her eyes. She looked like she could snap at any moment. With the kind of tips she probably made in this place, it was a surprise she didn't.

Danny sat at the bar alone, slowly drinking another Shiner. Loki had told him to relax, and Danny planned on doing just that. A Thursday night out on the town seemed like just the thing. He would enjoy himself, relax, and rest up for his next trip into Hell. He had waited this long to gather the stones. A few more days weren't going to make much of a difference.

He was on his third beer when nature called. As he stood in the small line to wait for his turn at the trough, he caught a glimpse of someone at the shuffleboard table. He couldn't see the face, only shoulder length red hair flipping in the neon light. He tried to push the thought out of his mind. How many red-heads were in the world anyway?

As he walked out of the restroom, he saw her face, if only briefly. It was definitely her. The girl from the mirror. She had a glistening sheen of sweat on her forehead and her hair swung as she turned. And walked right out the door.

Danny pushed his way through the small crowd and made his way out to the parking lot. It was empty. She was gone. He ran back inside.

He approached the guys at the table and yelled to be heard over the music, ZZ Top this time. "Hey!" he yelled. "Anybody know who that girl was?"

The three guys at the table looked at him for a minute, as if trying to decide if they should jump this guy for bothering them. Finally, two of them turned back to their game. The third shook his head.

"Sorry, dude. Girl came in and played a couple of games and took off. Didn't talk much." With that, he turned back to watch his friends.

Danny hung his head and walked back out into the parking lot, trying to figure out what to do next. Who knows how long he would've stood there if he hadn't seen the figure out of the corner of his eye. He turned to look, and there sitting on the curb was Loki, happily chomping away at his cigar.

"Hey there, Danny-boy," the imp said with a grin. "Fancy seeing you here."

Danny sat next to him. "What are you doing here?"

"I need a ride."

"How did you even get here? You're far too lazy to walk it," Danny asked.

"Ah," Loki responded, shaking a finger at him. "Never underestimate the kindness of strangers."

Danny nodded. "So you hitched?"

"Pretty much, yeah."

"And why did you come here?"

"Figured this is where you'd be. You always like to start your night at this place."

Danny sighed and had to let out a laugh. "Okay, where do you need to go?"

"Oh, no, no, no," Loki said. "The question is, 'Where do *we* need to go?'"

"No offense, Loki, but I'm not really in the mood. Something weird is-"

"Yeah, I don't really care," Loki cut him off. "You and I are going to hang out. I have a good feeling about tonight."

"Loki, I just saw the girl. The one in the mirror. I think someone's trying to get me to help her."

"Great. Did you talk to her?"

"No, she disappeared."

"Get a name?"

"Nothing."

Loki clapped his hands. "Aha. Well then, nothing can be done about it. If you're destined to help her, I'm sure you'll see her again soon. Until then..."

Danny shrugged. "Okay, where are we going?"

"Where else? We're headed downtown."

The two cruised the streets of Austin, neither saying much. The night had turned almost unbearably warm. Danny had the top of the car down, the sounds of Black Cat Rebellion blasting through the radio. The perfect music for a hot Austin night.

Danny had to park on the street, about four blocks from 6th Street, the center of Austin's nightlife. He and Loki picked their way through bumper to bumper traffic and past the barricades police had set up to close off downtown, like they did every busy bar night. The two turned the corner into a mass of people.

6th Street could be compared to Beale Street in Memphis, only, Danny thought, with better music. No surprise there. Everyone in Austin was an artist.

As they walked, the braver women stared and whistled at Danny. He was used to this by now. He was apparently an extremely attractive guy. He hated it sometimes, but that was just how God made him.

Loki nudged him in the ribs. "Gonna pull tonight?" he asked.

Danny shook his head. "I'm not really interested in a one night stand."

"Who said anything about a night? I'm talking about a few hours at most." Loki was in high spirits this evening.

Danny followed him down the street, already knowing where they were going. When Loki wanted a night out, there was only one place they would go: The Blind Pig, a two-story place that always featured live music. They got to the Pig and were waved in without even having their ID's checked. The doormen knew them all too well.

Loki almost slipped on the wet concrete floor, the spilled drinks already beginning to amass. A throng of people were making their way up the stairs to the rooftop. Behind the bar, a guy who looked like a young Gary Busey was wearing a cowboy hat and pouring drinks. For all Danny knew, it *was* Gary Busey, with a lot of surgery. He saw the two of them and nodded, turning to get their usual drinks. Joe Vega was just finishing up his first set of the night, just him and his guitar and a mike, pushed back against the wall so the crowd could get through to the back of the bar. Danny liked Joe quite a bit, not just for his musical talent, but because he was genuinely a nice guy. He was in his mid-30's, playing at this place six nights a week. Every night was the same thing. Joe would pass out a sheet with two hundred songs on it. After getting up and playing a few songs, he would ask the audience for requests, the audience just yelling out the name of a song, or the number on the paper, and Joe would play it from memory. It was impressive.

Joe finished off his last few chords and went to set his guitar down. A drunk girl at the end of the bar wearing a sundress, her black hair looking disheveled, kept calling out for Joe to play "Purple Rain", but he ignored her and walked towards the bar, saying hello to people he knew as he went. Danny and Loki got their drinks from the Busey look-a-like, and were just turning back when Danny felt a slap on the back.

"Hey, Danny! How're ya man?" Joe asked him.

"Not too bad," was Danny's reply.

"Good, good. Glad to see you out again." With that, Joe started to walk away.

Danny called after him. "Hey, Joe! When you going to learn some Who songs?"

Joe turned back and laughed. This was a running joke with them. "Soon as you start paying me, I'll learn."

Danny waved him off and turned back to his Red Bull and vodka while Joe got accosted by the drunk girl. He was feeling good. Loki was right. If he was really supposed to help the girl, destiny would intervene, but until then he would try to relax and prepare for his mission.

With Joe taking a break, the two headed upstairs to see who was playing on the roof. A jazz trio was just getting warmed up, and though they didn't interest Danny, Loki saw two girls near the stage that he was apparently interested in. He waved to Danny and took off in their direction.

Danny started to make his way to the edge of the roof. He loved the view from up here. Watching all the people walking down below always helped put things in perspective for him.

When he was just a few feet from it, and clear from the crowd around the stage, he was bumped in the side. His nearly full drink went spilling around his feet, a bit of it getting on him.

"Oh! Oh, man, I'm so, so sorry," came the voice from beside him. "I can buy you another if you want."

He turned, and there she was.

The girl with the red hair. The girl in the mirror. Destiny just loves to intervene when you least expect it.

Danny stared for what seemed an eternity. Unlike the vision he saw, this time he was able to take in every detail about the girl. Fiery red hair, green eyes that sparkled like emeralds, questioning and trying to read him. Soft, pale skin, not porcelain, but smooth like butter-cream. He was entranced by her beauty. Which is exactly what pulled him out. Danny's mind knew far better than his body that he shouldn't be enthralled like that. He snapped back to reality as the girl was speaking.

"Okay," she said, shaking her head. "So, no drink then. Sorry about bumping into you."

She turned and began walking back towards the door to the stairs. Danny knew that he was probably just asking for trouble getting involved in whatever this was while he had so much going on elsewhere, but he decided to do it anyway.

"Wait," he called out after her, making up the distance between them in just a few steps. He grabbed her arm to stop her. Without looking at him, she looked at his hand holding her arm, a trace of anger in her face.

"Sorry," he said, immediately releasing her arm. "I was just..."

She gave a curt nod, still avoiding looking directly at him. "Yeah. I bet that happens a lot."

"Sometimes, I guess. Look, I'm really sorry, I space out occasionally. But I think I would like that drink," he said.

She sighed, trying to buy herself time while making her decision. "Alright, I guess I do owe you," she said, "but just the one."

Danny followed as she turned, her mind made up now. Moving quickly and gracefully, she picked her way through the crowd to the stairs, then back down into the darkness of the bar's interior. On his way, he gave a cursory glance towards Loki, who was heavily engaged in entertaining the two girls.

Danny picked his way to the bar, where the

girl had already managed to find an open spot and gotten the bartender's attention. He noticed Joe was in the corner with the drunk girl hanging all over him. Just another night in Texas.

The girl nodded at Danny, and Not Gary Busey looked at him in surprise. "Already?"

"Accident," Danny explained, handing the empty glass over the bar.

Not Gary Busey looked from Danny to the girl and back again. "Oh, I'm sure." He turned and began filling Danny's glass. While waiting, Danny tried to inconspicuously look at the girl. She was smiling to herself while watching Joe struggle with the girl. The bartender handed Danny's drink to him. The girl slid a twenty across.

"So, what are you drinking, big man?" she asked.

"Red bull and vodka," Danny answered, feeling the vodka burn the back of his throat. Not Gary Busey made this one quite a bit stronger than the first.

The girl gave a smirk and rolled her eyes a bit. "Aren't you trendy?" she asked, the sarcasm dripping off her words.

"Nope," Danny answered. "Just happen to like it." The girl nodded and pocketed the change the bartender handed to her. "I didn't get your name," Danny added. So far, he wasn't getting any sort of vibe from this girl, but that didn't necessarily mean anything. The vision might have been some future incident. He needed to investigate further.

"Look, I'm not really looking for some deep,

soul-searching bar conversation. So, I've apologized, you have your drink, and now I bid you a good night," she said, giving a little curtsy and the end.

"Sorry, I wasn't trying to start anything," Danny said. "I just wanted to know who to thank for the drink."

"I have a boyfriend." It was the type of automatic answer that comes with years of having to deal with guys hitting on her. It was enough to make Danny feel a bit bad for her and laugh at the same time.

"Does he not let you have a name?" Danny asked. He definitely liked this girl. She had a tough streak and wasn't afraid to show it. Him not backing down from it was enough to garner a smile from her.

"Elizabeth," she said. It fit her, Danny thought. Very old world. "But my friends call me Liz."

Danny reached out to shake her hand. "It's nice to meet you, Liz."

She shook her head. "Never said we were friends," she said, a bit of a mischievous look in her eyes. She was enjoying herself, even if only a little. Danny had that affect on people.

"Sorry," Danny said, bowing his head a bit. "My name's Daniel. My friends call me Danny."

"Well, it's a pleasure to meet you, Danny."

"Ah, so I'm guessing we're friends now?" he asked, smiling.

"Yeah, well..." she paused, looked around the bar, seemingly trying to make a decision. "It's been real and all." She started to walk away. Danny tried racking his brain to think of a way to keep her from leaving.

"You're not going to let me drink all alone, are you?" he asked. Even he knew it smacked of desperation, but he couldn't let her go quite yet. Red hair and a first name were not enough to go on when it came to investigating a girl who showed up in a vision in his shower. He needed more. And frankly, he was interested in her, even though he truly didn't want to be. She fascinated and frightened him a bit.

Liz hesitated. That was good enough for Danny. She was considering the idea of staying and talking. He would take all he could get.

She looked to the door again, and came to her decision. "I'm sure an attractive guy like you could find someone to talk to." She smiled while she said it though.

"Possibly," Danny countered. "But why deny fate? Perhaps you bumped into me for a reason."

Liz laughed, her entire body consumed with the humor. "Yeah," she said. "You were in my way." Danny noted she wasn't looking at the door anymore.

"Okay, so there was that too. And just why were you so anxious to get to the edge of the roof?"

She shrugged. "I was hoping to spot someone. I'm guessing they're gone by now," she said.

"So you're not in a hurry anymore?"

"I guess not," she said.

"I promise, I won't keep you long," he said, giving her what he hoped was a reassuring smile. To further re-enforce his point, he drained half of his drink. "So, what do you do, Elizabeth?"

"I'm a nurse."

Danny nodded. "That sounds interesting."

"It's really, really not."

"So why do it then?"

Liz pursed her lips in thought for a moment, finally shrugging, not seeming to find a decent answer. "I don't know. I guess I couldn't figure out much else to do with a major in Latin."

"Ah. I do so love Latin," Danny said. As soon as he said it, he realized how stupid it sounded. No one loved Latin. It was something you said if you couldn't come up with any other bad pick-up lines.

Liz seemed to be thinking the same thing. The change came over her face almost instantly, the change that comes from thinking a pleasant conversation has just turned into serious flirting.

"Okay, I've really got to go now," she said, once again starting to leave. Danny resisted the urge to reach out and grab her again.

"Wait, look...," he said, but she was already on the move.

Without looking back, she said loudly enough so that he could hear her over the murmurs of the crowd, "I told you, I have a boyfriend. And now I have to go." With that, she immediately headed towards the door and out into the night.

Danny stood for a split second, trying to decide what to do. He could let her go, and maybe whatever was supposed to happen would happen. Maybe he wasn't supposed to figure it all out tonight. Or maybe it would be best just to leave the whole thing alone, and worry more about planning his next trip into Hell and gathering the stones. But his body was already in motion. He downed his drink and was headed towards the door before he even realized he was doing it. The stones had waited this long; they could wait a little while longer. He wanted to know who this girl was, and why he was so taken with her.

Danny emerged from the bar into the neon lights and crowd of 6th Street. A quick glance to his left was all he needed to find Liz, her red hair glimmering in the lights. He pushed through the crowd after her, hoping he would figure out something decent to say to her by the time he reached her. The crowd was thick enough that he had to work his way slowly, bumping into people occasionally and offering apologies along the way. He never took his eyes off Liz, following her as she turned down an alley. By the time he had reached the mouth of the alley, he saw her almost a block ahead. He decided against yelling after her, not wanting to spook her. No matter what happened, he figured he was going to look crazy. There was no reason to seem any crazier than he had to.

She turned a corner again onto 4th Street, and Danny turned as well, a few steps behind.

"Hey," he said. That was the best he had been able to come up with. He really didn't have anything to follow it with either.

Liz rounded on him, eyes wide in anger and disbelief. "What the hell? Are you following me?" she asked, trying hard to maintain her cool.

Danny simply shrugged. "Sort of," he answered sheepishly.

"Unbelievable," she turned and walked, her pace quickened and exaggerated with her anger.

"Look, I know this is a bit weird," Danny said, trying to match her pace. It was much easier to keep up with her now. The street was completely empty, other than the cars parked along the curb.

"A bit weird?" she stopped, hand reaching instinctively towards her pocket, where Danny imagined she kept mace or some sort of protection. She made sure to keep a safe distance between them, a few feet, with a fire hydrant between the two.

"Okay, it's a lot weird," Danny admitted, "but, please, at least hear me out."

She eased up a bit. "What could you possibly have to say? I told you I have a boyfriend."

"I know, I know," Danny said. He was trying to find just the right thing to say, but it wasn't easy. Something seemed off. Not with the conversation, that was going to seem odd no matter what. It was the emptiness of the street. Something about it bothered him. Liz noticed him taking in the empty street, and her hand shot back to her pocket, tensing up.

"Whoa, buddy. Whatever is on your mind, I think you should just take a step back, and walk away."

"Huh?" Danny asked. It took a moment to register what she was insinuating. "Oh, no," he said, almost matter of factly. "I don't want to rape you or anything."

"That's reassuring," Liz said, pulling her hand from her pocket, this time removing the small object she carried with her. A collapsible baton. If Danny wasn't preoccupied, he would have appreciated her idea of protection.

"Really, I don't mean you any harm. It's just that I had... I mean, there's something..." he struggled. Something was definitely wrong here. "I just... do you want to get some coffee? I have something I think we should discuss."

Liz opened the baton with a flick of her wrist. "Are you serious? No, I don't want to have coffee with you. Seriously, whatever your deal is, just leave me alone."

Danny knew what was about to happen the moment the stench of sulfur hit his nose. "We need to get off the street. Now!" he yelled. It was too late.

Before Liz could answer, the fire hydrant between them exploded, knocking them both back in a spray of water.

Danny was up in a heartbeat, frantically searching through the water spray for either Liz or the attacker. It was Liz he saw first. The poor girl was completely soaked. Danny assumed he was too, but he didn't feel anything at the moment. He was running on instinct.

Danny grabbed her under her arms and drug her behind a nearby car, just as another blast rained down near them. He peered over the hood of the car, trying to see who was firing at them. He thought it had to be coming from the alley across the street. It was dark and shadowy, the perfect place for someone to hide.

Liz looked at him dumbfounded. "What the hell was that?" she asked.

"Pretty appropriate question," Danny answered. He could hear footsteps coming from the alley. Not just one attacker, but at least a half dozen. He risked another look, only to see seven creatures leaving the alley and spilling into the street.

"Turagios. Great." Danny looked at Liz. "I need you to stay down and out of the way," he said. He hesitated for a moment, as if trying to think of something else to say. Instead he grabbed the baton from her. "Need to borrow this for a moment."

He made his way to the edge of the car and took one more look. The creatures in the street, Turagios, were ugly mothers. Each one stood close to seven feet, thick brown hides covered by patchwork leather armor. And each carried a long, double-edged knife. They weren't what worried Danny though. Turagios could be beaten easily. It was the sniper Danny was concerned with. Turagios had no interest in magic. Someone else was firing off the blasts.

Another blast hit the front of the car, shaking it. Danny decided now was the time to make his move. He ran at the nearest creature, hitting it where its neck and shoulders met with the baton, then hitting its forearm. He heard bones in the arm crack and the knife dropped. Danny grabbed the knife and dropped the baton, jabbing the knife into the Turagio's neck.

The other creatures closed on him swiftly, while the sniper in the alley fired another blast.

Danny made a quick turn, the blast narrowly missing him. He turned right into the next Turagio and shoved the knife through the flimsy armor and into the creature's chest. It gave an excited grunt and fell to the ground, yellow ooze spraying from its chest wound into the open air.

Danny ducked a slash from the third Turagio, close enough to this one to see the snot dripping from it's snout-like nose. He was running out of time and space. The others were closing in on him. He snapped the third creature's neck with a quick flourish. He grabbed this one's knife, holding one in each hand, and threw them at the next two approaching creatures. He caught each in the forehead, dropping them instantly.

With no more weapons in hand and two Turagios left, Danny made a mad dash across the street. He was hoping his kamikaze technique would work on the sniper.

Liz was still crouched behind the car, looking over the trunk, utterly shocked. This guy had just cut through a group of pig-looking creatures, and someone was shooting what looked to be bolts of fire. The other two creatures had almost reached Danny, who was scrambling desperately towards the alley. Whoever was in the alley fired off a few more of the fire bolts, missing each time, as Danny zigged and zagged his way towards the sniper. Just as Danny reached the alley, the two remaining pig creatures disappeared in a plume of yellowish smoke. Liz shook her head, trying to force her brain to make sense of what she was seeing. It didn't seem to work.

Danny reached the mouth of the alley. Standing just a few feet away, partially hidden in shadows, stood another demon, a Ra'al. This caused Danny a moment's pause, his mind filling swiftly with possibilities. Turagios and Ra'als hated each other. Why would they be here on Earth, working together? If the Ra'al had chosen, he probably could have struck Danny with a blast from his long wooden staff right then. But he did nothing, simply watching Danny. This creature, unlike the Turagio's, looked vaguely human, if a human's skin looked like melting wax. He was sallow and wrinkly, dressed in a dark, hooded cloak, and holding his staff, a glowing blood-red crystal perched atop it. Danny understood this was where the blasts were coming from, the source of all the creature's power.

Danny advanced on it, grabbing the Ra'al by the cloak, and throwing it against the wall. "Know that I give my life willingly, and-" the Ra'al started to say, but Danny stopped him.

"I don't want to kill you," Danny growled at it. "What are you doing here? How did you find me?"

The Ra'al laughed and looked at the amulet around Danny's neck. "Your bobble didn't work? It would appear things are not as they seem, are they?"

"You're not answering my question."

"I'm not here to answer to the likes of you, fallen one," the creature spat at him. Danny wiped his face quickly, while the Ra'al went on. "I am simply a messenger."

"Fine," Danny said, irritated. "What's the message?"

"The Lords of Hell have noted your trespasses. They are displeased." The Ra'al gave a sick smile. Danny wanted nothing more than to demolish its face.

"I have a message for your Lords. Tell them that-" Danny didn't have time to finish. The Ra'al slammed his staff against the ground, disappearing in a thick cloud of yellowish smoke and sulfur smell. Danny instinctively stepped back. He stared at the empty alley a moment longer. Realizing it was over, he ran his hands through his hair and sighed. "Damn," was all he could think to say. This just wasn't his day.

Danny re-emerged from the alley. He crossed the street, stopping only to pick up the baton. Liz was still crouched behind the car, seemingly in shock. He tried to hand the baton back to her, but she didn't take it, simply staring at him instead. She was completely soaked and shivering.

Not thinking of anything else good to say, Danny gave a sheepish grin and asked, "So, how about that coffee?"

The Book of Daniel

Interlude
The American Southwest

The American desert is a beautiful place, but it can be dangerous. The creatures that live there have adapted to survive, often in lethal ways.

The two creatures walking hand in hand under the full desert moon were as lethal as they come.

Their names were Bob and Jezebel. Long, scraggly hair hung to the shoulders of both. They were dirty, dusty, looking almost like something from a time long since passed. The moonlight made their pale skin look porcelain white. The only thing that stood out in the pale light was their eyes, bright, shining, and dancing. They walked, Jezebel aimlessly, Bob with a purpose. And they were hungry, oh so hungry.

"Bob?" Jezebel asked. She was sleepy. There hadn't been much in the desert to keep her belly full or keep her occupied. She had none of the manic life in her that she would have if they'd stayed in the city like she wanted. She loved the city. So many people, so much fun. Bob wasn't much for the city though. He preferred to keep to the edges of civilization. "Where we goin', baby?"

Bob continued walking for a moment, staring thoughtfully at the moon. "Utah," he finally said, as if that were answer enough.

Jezebel giggled. "Utah? Why? Ain't nothing but Mormons in Utah."

"Nah, there's something else there," Bob answered.

Jezebel stopped walking and dropped his hand. "What, baby? What's so great in Utah?"

"I don't know," he said, never taking his eyes off the moon.

"You don't know?" she asked, throwing a mock pouty face at him. "Let's go to the coast. I want to see me some movie stars." Her face immediately brightened at this prospect.

Bob stopped looking at the moon and cast his gaze onto her. Her smile disappeared. There was a fire in his eyes that frightened her sometimes. Bob knew things that others didn't, and she didn't like it. She didn't like the idea that there might be something out there bigger than them. That scared her.

"I don't know, baby. I don't know what's in Utah," Bob told her, taking both her hands in his. "I just know we need to go. The whispers are tellin' me that's where we need to go." He nodded at the moon, to make sure she understood. The night whispered to Bob, deep, dark voices that frightened him sometimes, but also gave him a purpose. It was those voices that told him to find Jezebel in the first place. That was over a hundred years ago, and they'd been some of the best of his life. He wasn't about to start doubting them now.

"Okay," she said, hesitantly. "If they say we need to go, I guess we go."

He pulled her close and held her for a moment,

smelling the earth, the dust of the great American expanse on her hair. He released her and stared into her eyes once more.

"I promise, things will be good," he said. "I got a vague idea where to go. We need to pay a visit to a man. And then, baby, then we get to have some fun."

Her face brightened once again at this. "Will there be food?" she asked.

"Of course there will, baby. So much food. And so, so much blood. We'll swim in it."

She gave a squeal and hugged him. The voices scared her, but the voices always took them to something good, eventually.

"Time's comin', baby," he said. "Time's comin', they keep telling me, that all this will be ours. It's almost our time, and the world's ours. And the world will burn."

Bob and Jezebel interlocked their fingers and resumed their walking.

Desert creatures are sometimes the most dangerous of all.

The Book of Daniel

3

*In which Danny and Liz get coffee,
introductions are made, and Danny
is surprised yet again.*

Danny and Liz sat across from each other, her staring down at her hands in her lap, him staring at her expectantly. The little diner they were in was almost completely empty, which was a good thing, as two people soaked to the bone might have made a scene otherwise. The buzzing fluorescents didn't help things. Liz, in particular, looked quite disheveled.

The waitress brought out two cups of coffee, and though Danny gave her an appreciative nod, she didn't look twice at them. This was Austin. She was all too used to weirdness.

Danny took a gulp of the hot coffee and continued staring at Liz, who did absolutely nothing. "You should drink," he finally said. "It will help. Warm you up and all that."

She finally looked at him, her face twisted in confusion and slight anger. She started to speak once, and stopped, content to simply stare back at him for a moment.

"Okay," Danny said, more to break the uncomfortable silence than anything. "I know this is probably all a bit strange."

"Who are you?" she asked.

"I'm Danny."

"Danny who?"

"Just Danny."

Her eyes narrowed in suspicion. "You don't have a last name?"

"Not normally," he shrugged.

"How do you not have a last name? How do you have a house, or apartment, or job, or car without a last name?"

"It's complicated," he answered.

"Make it simple for me then," she demanded.

Danny sighed. This line of questioning wasn't going to help any. "Maybe we should start with something less complicated," he suggested.

"You said you had something you thought we should discuss. What was it?" she asked.

"That's... that's really not any easier to explain," he said. She glared at him. "I could try, though," he said, not wanting to anger or irritate her any-more than possible. "This is going to seem very strange to you."

"I just saw you fight a bunch of ugly pig-look-ing...things. Right now, I'm surrounded in strange. Try me."

"Okay, I...um...," Danny stammered trying to think of the best way to proceed. He hated this part of the job, the part where he had to get into the details of his strange little world. He much preferred moments like earlier, when things just jumped out and he dealt with them. On second thought, no, he really didn't like that part either.

"Are you in any sort of trouble?" he finally asked.

"Trouble?" she repeated. "Like what?"

"I don't know. Any kind. Like, is there any-one after you or anything?" he asked. Not having details was always a drawback with visions.

"Sure," she answered. "The student loan people call everyday. What the hell does that have to do with anything?"

"So, no one trying to physically harm you though?"

"No," she answered. "What, are you a cop or something?"

"Not really. Look, I'm just going to come out and say this, no matter how insane it sounds. I had a vision of you, and in the vision you were in trouble." He sat looking at her, waiting for a response. She wasn't laughing yet, so that was a good start.

Liz processed the information. "So," she finally said, slowly, "you have visions, but no last name?"

Danny had to laugh at that. It was probably the best reaction he'd ever had to the insane circumstances of his existence. "I lead a very odd life," he answered.

Liz started to play with her coffee cup, still not taking a drink, but at least Danny thought she seemed to be loosening up a little bit.

"What kind of trouble was I in, in this vision of yours?" she asked.

"You don't think I'm crazy?" Danny asked, a bit surprised.

"Oh, you're definitely crazy," Liz said. "But after what I just saw, I'm willing to give crazy a chance."

"Fair enough. I don't know what kind of trouble it was. I just know you were in trouble."

"How do you know that?" she asked. "Just... I guess, just tell me what it was you saw?"

"I saw your face," Danny said. Now it was his turn to play with his cup.

"That's it? How do you know I was in trouble?"

"There was... you... you were beaten. Bleeding. Someone had done a number on you," he looked up, hoping maybe she might now have a clue what this was about.

"Nothing else? That's all you saw?" she asked. Danny nodded. "Could it have been those things? Those pig guys from earlier?"

"No, they were after me." And that's a whole other mystery, Danny thought to himself. There was suddenly too much piling up so swiftly around him.

"Why were they after you?" Liz asked. She picked up her cup and took a drink, face grimacing a little at the heat of the drink. But at least she seemed calm.

"That's a long story," Danny said.

"I've got time."

"I don't really think it ties in to your situation."

"Well, since I have no idea who would want to beat me, and I'm a bit terrified to go out into the street again, why don't you go ahead and fill me in."

Danny despised talking about himself. It always made him feel uneasy, as his ex-wives would all openly admit, if they could. Besides, telling Liz too much would be a bad thing. If she knew too much about the world that lay just below the surface of her own, if she started to glimpse some of the truths that most humans ignored, she could be in grave danger. For the first time, Danny began to wonder if perhaps *he* could be responsible for the beating she had taken in his vision. A self-fulfilling prophecy perhaps? It wouldn't be the first time.

"It's not a big deal, really," he finally said. "They just don't like me much."

"Really?" she laughed. "I couldn't tell from their giant knives and pissed off expressions."

Danny smiled at that. "You're taking this a lot better than I expected," he admitted.

Liz shrugged. "At this point, I'm just trying to roll with it. Tomorrow, I'll probably write the whole thing off to hallucinations stemming from bad yogurt or something." She took a deep drink from her cup, then resettled herself in her seat and looked at Danny, deeply, inquisitively. "No last name, visions, angry pig-people. Just what is it you do, stranger?" Before Danny could answer, she added, "And none of this 'It's complicated' bull. Straight answer. I think I deserve that, at least."

"Yeah," Danny nodded. "You probably do. But it is complicated," he added. Liz laughed at that. "Honestly, what I do isn't all that exciting. I'm mainly just a collector. The fighting only happens every now and then."

Liz stared at him for a moment, trying to decipher his answer. "Are you wanted or anything?"

"Wanted?"

"Yeah, by the authorities. Like, are you a criminal or something?"

"No. Why would you ask that?" Danny said. He was a bit infatuated with Liz, even though he knew once her adrenaline dropped back to normal levels she would become much more clear-headed and less enthused about all the mystery.

"I'm sorry," she said. "I don't mean any disrespect by it. It's just, usually when someone says they're a collector, they're either a thief or really into comic books or baseball cards."

"Met a lot of thieves?" Danny asked with a wry grin.

"I work in the ER," she answered. "You'd be surprised who I meet."

Danny thought about that for a moment and nodded. "Nothing that exciting, I'm afraid. I'm the boring kind of collector."

"Oh, I know all about those. So what do you collect?" she asked.

"Right now, stones," he shrugged. "Like I said, boring."

She gave a curious smile. "You have no idea how interesting this is to me right now." A quizzical look crossed Danny's face. "What kind of stones are you collecting? Diamonds, rubies, emeralds? If so, I'd have to start wondering if you're a thief again."

"I doubt you'd have any idea what I was talking about. They're not your typical geological stones."

"Okay, that rules out digging in the desert. And you said stones, not bones, so you're not a paleontologist. So, come on, spill it. What do you collect?"

Danny felt something stirring, some small change in the atmosphere. He was having that feeling that, somewhere, things were starting to click into place, like a gear was beginning to turn.

"Well," he started, cautiously, trying to gauge her reaction, "right now, I'm collecting a group of stones called the Terrarum Exstinctor Stones."

Liz put her coffee cup down and looked at Danny. Neither said anything, both simply staring at the other. Danny was beginning to formulate a possible reason why he had gotten the vision, and he didn't like it one bit. Everything was far too connected.

"The World Destroyer Stones?" Liz asked. "Are we talking about the same thing?"

Danny's breath caught in his throat. "What do you know about them?" he asked.

"Not much," she admitted. "I know there's nineteen of them." Danny nodded. This, at least, was good. If that's all she knew, then she truly didn't know the danger of them. It also meant she hadn't been fully brought into the circles that made up Danny's world. He didn't know why, but more than anything, he wanted to keep her away from that world. It would be safer for her here, in the everyday human world, where a bump in the night was still nothing more than a bump.

Danny took a drink of his coffee, but Liz continued. "I also know where eight of them are." Danny almost spit out his coffee.

"You want to run that by me again?" he asked.

"I know where eight of them are," Liz answered. Danny stared at her in disbelief. "I take it they're not easy to find," she said.

Danny continued to stare.

"I knew they were kind of important, but I

didn't think they were that big of a deal," she continued, seeing the look on Danny's face, and realizing that they were, in fact, a very big deal.

A million thoughts raced through Danny's head at once. There were nineteen stones. He had ten of them. With the eight she knew of, and the one in Hell, he would have them all. He could finally put an end to this whole mess. He could finally leave the last two hundred years in the past.

Something had to go wrong though. He knew that from his vision. Once again, the stones wouldn't come without a price.

"Where... how...," Danny struggled to find the right question. "How do you even know about these?"

Liz laughed. "Like I kept trying to tell you, I have a boyfriend." Danny nodded, not quite understanding. Liz went on regardless. "He's an antiques dealer here in town. Always on the lookout for the rarest of the rare. Mostly, it's just crappy rugs and stuff he sells to tourists, but his real passion is in ancient artifacts."

"So, he just went out and found these?"

"Some of them. A few of them came from his family. His father was a collector too."

Danny thought long and hard. He knew exactly what he needed to do, but he didn't know if Liz's boyfriend would go for it. If the guy knew what he had, Danny was sure he was probably very cautious with them.

"You want to meet him now, don't you?" Liz asked, as if she was reading his mind.

It seemed like it might work out much easier than Danny thought. Whether that was a good or bad thing remained to be seen.

The Book of Daniel

4

In which good vibes are crushed, a plan begins to form, and Danny and Loki earn a paycheck.

Danny opened the door to the rundown apartment in a better mood than he'd been in a long, long time. The sun had been up for a few hours, but he was just getting home. He had spent the entire night in Zilker Park, just trying to believe his sudden turn of good luck.

He was whistling quietly to himself, when he stopped with a smile on his face. Loki stood on a chair in front of the coffee maker, hunched over, head on the counter top. With a wicked grin, Danny rushed over, picked him up, and spun him around.

"Good morning, you beautiful imp," Danny said. He sat Loki back down on the floor. Loki stared at him, bleary eyed and unhappy.

"I'm moments away from puking on your shoes, you right git," the imp said.

Danny laughed. It felt good. Everything felt good right now. "I keep telling you to cut back on the booze."

"I like booze," Loki responded. "You? Not so much right now." Loki looked at him for a moment. "What's got in to you?" he finally asked.

"I found the girl," Danny said, stealing the first cup of coffee before Loki could climb back on the chair.

"Super. Save her from the big bad and all that?"

"Not quite," Danny said, gulping his coffee.

"Then why so chipper?" A look crossed Loki's face. "Danny, did you and that girl..."

"Of course not, we just met."

Loki shrugged. "Your loss." He managed to get up on the chair, but had to pause once there. After a few deep breaths, he grabbed a cup and filled it. "So what's the big deal then? I haven't seen you this happy since...what, Russia, maybe?"

"I wasn't happy, I was drugged," Danny answered.

"Yeah, we really made those witches mad."

Danny nodded. "That's what happens when you sick the Inquisition on someone." Danny continued grinning. The sunlight streaming in through the kitchen window was the perfect accent to his mood. Loki simply stood, waiting. "I found them," Danny said finally.

"Found what?"

"The rest of the stones. I found them. Right here in town."

Loki dropped his cup and stared dumbly.

"Yeah, that was pretty much my reaction," Danny said. He grabbed a broom from the corner and quickly swept up the broken shards. Loki grabbed his shoulders and stopped him before he could clean up the coffee.

"Are you sure? This is real?"

"Yeah, it is." Danny removed the imp's hands and bent down to clean up the spilled coffee.

"The girl has a boyfriend. He's an antiques collector. And he just happens to have the last eight stones."

Loki nodded. "So we're doing a smash and grab job?"

"No," Danny said. He paused, unsure if Loki would understand. "We're going to do this one legit."

"Why? If this guy has eight stones, he surely knows what he has. I doubt he's going to be willing to part with them."

"I know that. I don't know," Danny shrugged, "I guess... I guess I just want to see how things are before we go and do it the hard way."

"You sure that's it?" Loki asked.

"What else would it be?"

"The girl?"

"It has nothing to do with the girl," Danny scoffed. "It would just be nice to not have to fight for things for once."

"We've been fighting for a long time. We've only just started making real progress the last few years. Just seems hard to believe it would be so easy all of a sudden," Loki said. He stood thinking for a moment, before a troubled look crossed his face. "Wait," he said. "You said this bloke has eight of the stones."

Danny finished cleaning up the coffee and stood. "Yeah," he simply said.

"Well, by my calculations, Daniel, that still leaves us one short," Loki said. Danny nodded at this. "It's the stone we've been after, isn't it?" Danny nodded again. "You have to go to Hell again, don't you? Damn, I was hoping we'd get lucky on that one."

"I would have had to go anyway. We're never that lucky," Danny said. It was a thought he didn't relish, and it was the one downside to all this. No matter how good the news was, there was still the matter of Hell. "Even without these eight, we knew I'd have to go back. Nothing's going to change that."

Loki sighed. "I'd prefer the smash and grab job. At least we can guess what might happen there. But Hell..."

"I know," Danny said. "But Hell isn't really that bad, if I can avoid the demons. And I'm going to take every precaution."

"Yes, you are," Loki agreed. "Because I'm going with you this time."

"No. No way. Not happening," Danny said firmly.

"Yes, it is. There's no way I'm letting you go back again alone."

"I'm not even sure you could survive the journey, let alone-"

Loki cut him off. "I'm a magical being," he said. "I've traveled to other realms before. That's not an issue. You're going to need all the help you can get. Do you even know exactly where the stone is down there?"

"I've narrowed it down to a general location."

"Good, then that settles it," Loki poured himself another cup of coffee. "I can help you find it, then get you out of there in one piece. It's too dangerous for you to be doing this completely on your own."

Danny begrudgingly agreed. "Fine," he said.

"But I'm in charge. You think you understand Hell? You have no idea. There's things down there that you wouldn't expect."

Loki laughed. "Have you forgotten the time I was swallowed and digested by a giant fish? I can handle pain and torture."

Danny gave him an odd look. "You don't even know torture until you've stepped through the gates of Hell." With that, Danny started towards his bedroom to get some rest. His good mood had been completely dampened.

"Oh, by the way," Loki said, "all of this is going to have to wait a bit."

"Why's that?"

"Well, stones or no stones, we got a call for a job. Real nasty one too, from the sound of it," Loki told him. He pointed to a note hung on the refrigerator. Danny inspected the note and sighed.

"Okay, guess we'd better take care of this. Too bad. I was hoping to have a little time to relax," Danny told him. "Clients pay upfront?"

"They promised a check in the mail tomorrow," Loki answered.

"Right, then. Time to go slay a dragon."

It wasn't a dragon, not really, but it was close enough for Danny to wonder if perhaps these creatures had helped spread the myths of dragons. Of course, there were real dragons in existence as well, they just hadn't been seen on Earth since well before the 9th century.

This creature, from what Danny understood, was an Ebulba, not a particularly nasty creature, but a danger all the same. From what Danny could remember of them, they were demons summoned to take out an enemy. The problems arose after they took out their target. Ebulbas didn't want to go back from whatever realm they were called out of. They seemed to like Earth, and would simply chose to stay, often killing and taking over the residency of whomever had called them. Even this wouldn't have been too much of an issue with Danny, if it didn't include the fact that the favorite meal of the Ebulba was human children. That tended to give Danny an unfavorable view of a creature.

They drove to an empty housing addition near Round Rock, just north of Austin. Since it was a weekend, the place stood empty. Large gates stood out front, telling Danny that this was soon to be another of the gated communities around Austin, built for rich executives in a town getting a reputation as 'Little Silicon Valley.'

"Who called us on this?" Danny asked.

"The future homeowner," Loki told him. "He got our number from one of the construction guys. Workers had called him about a disturbance, and he showed up to find this thing sitting where his foundation was supposed to be poured. Of course, none of the construction guys were going to mess with it."

"Can't blame them for that. Any idea where this place is?"

"Yeah, guy said it would be just... There, it's that one, with the granite wall running around it," Loki said.

Danny laughed. "Even in a gated community, the guy wants to put up a wall around himself," he said.

They pulled up to the curb in front of the place, a lot that had nothing on it except the wall and a large hole in the ground. Danny reached into the glove box and pulled out his silver knife, something that seemed to defy the definition of a knife, as it was as long as a man's forearm and gleamed menacingly in the early morning light.

"Okay, from what you've told me about these things, they're not really violent creatures, right?" Loki asked.

"From what I remember, no, not unless they're provoked. Which we're probably going to do," he answered. "This is why I told you to bring the book."

Loki patted the book in his lap, a book so large it almost seemed as big as the imp itself. "Right, right," he said.

"How do we kill it?" Danny asked, opening the car door and listening. The creature wasn't making any sounds. Danny wasn't sure if that meant it was sleeping, or out hunting. He was hoping for sleeping.

Loki flipped open the book to a page he had marked with a bar receipt. "Um... looks like you just stab it in the heart."

"Okay, easy enough," Danny said. He got out of the car, and Loki followed suit, carrying the book with him. The two approached the property and stopped at the gate of the wall.

"I guess the thing that's bugging me," Loki started again, "if it's not really a violent creature, why do we have to kill it? I mean, can't we just relocate it or something? Find it a nice home in the wilderness, ya know?"

"It eats little kids, Loki!" Danny sighed and shook his head. "I'm not going to let something like that just wander around. I don't like killing living creatures, but some things just need to be put down.

"What about a spell then? Send it back to it's home or whatever?"

Danny laughed. "You try getting one of these to stand still long enough to draw a circle around it and do the right preparations," he said.

"Alright, fine. I just don't like taking a life before lunch."

The two started for the future site of the house. As they reached the pit, they could hear deep breathing, meaning the Ebulba was sleeping. Danny put his finger over his lips, telling Loki to stay quiet. They approached the dirt rampway, leading down into the pit and walked down it, slowly and quietly.

Once they had entered, they saw the creature, taking up quite a bit of what would eventually be a huge basement. The Ebulba was a dirty yellow color, roughly the size of a Mack truck. It was curled up and sleeping, its tail with twin spikes laying on top of its head, covering the creature's eyes. Danny could see razor sharp claws, four to each paw, and a narrow strip of bony protrusions running along its back. It was easy to see why people would have mistaken these for dragons years ago.

The one problem Danny saw was that, as the creature was sleeping on its belly, it would have to be woken to reach the heart. He sighed and looked around, spotting a large rock a few feet away. He picked the rock up and threw it, hitting the Ebulba directly on the nose.

"Hey! Hey, wake up, you scaly punk!" Danny yelled at it.

The Ebulba slowly stirred, its tail swishing back to its rear as it opened its coal black eyes. It looked at Danny with a curious interest, as if wondering who in their right mind would bother it while it was sleeping.

Danny grabbed another rock and threw it, hitting the Ebulba in the face again. That one got its attention.

The Ebulba got to its feet, moving slowly and precisely. It didn't need to rush. These two tiny things before it were obviously easy prey.

"Loki, grab me some more rocks, I don't care what size. I just need something to get it angry," Danny said.

Loki dropped the book and ran around gathering rocks, as the Ebulba stretched itself out. Danny was noticing that there was quickly becoming less and less room to maneuver in the pit.

Loki brought back a handful of medium sized rocks.

"Why, exactly, do we want it to be angry?" he asked.

"Just hoping for something," Danny responded.

Danny grabbed the first rock and threw it, hitting the Ebulba in the face. It opened its mouth to roar, and what came out sounded more like a high pitched squeal.

"What was that?" Loki asked.

"That's what they sound like," Danny said, picking up a second rock. "Not too tough, huh?"

Danny threw the second rock. The Ebulba used one of its paws to bat the rock out of the air. Danny smiled. He continued throwing the rocks, faster and faster. The Ebulba continued batting them down with its paws, until finally, getting tired of this little game, rose up on its rear haunches and gave another cry.

Danny took this opening, and launched himself at the creature's exposed chest. He drove the knife as hard as he could into the creature's heart, pulling the knife back and stabbing three times for good measure. The Ebulba gave a stifled cry, then fell on its back, Danny still clinging to it. He removed his blade and walked back to Loki.

"That wasn't too bad after all," Danny said. He produced a rag from his coat pocket and began cleaning the creature's green blood from the blade.

"Yeah, I thought-" Loki stopped mid-sentence and pointed to the Ebulba. "Um, are its eyes supposed to still be moving?"

Danny turned to look and saw that the creature's eyes were indeed still moving. On top of that, he realized it was still breathing.

"Loki, hand me the book," Danny said. Loki continued to stare at the the Ebulba, which was slowly starting to move. "Loki! Now!"

Loki quickly picked the book up and handed it to Danny. He opened it up to the place Loki had marked and read quickly.

"This isn't the page on Ebulba's," he said. "It's a Chinese fire dragon."

"Well, it looked like the description," Loki said sheepishly.

"Just because the picture's the same... did you even read the description?"

"You know I don't really know Latin," Loki told him.

"I... you...," Danny trailed off. He began flipping through the book, looking for the entry on the Ebulba. He found it, just as the creature was struggling to its feet. It fell back, shaking the earth. Danny was running out of time.

"Here it is," he said. "You have to cut off the head and salt the stump. Do we have any salt?"

"In the car," Loki said, already halfway back up the ramp.

"Get it. And bring me some gasoline, too," Danny yelled after him.

Danny dropped the book back on the ground and charged at the Ebulba. He was lucky that the the wound he gave the creature was enough to leave it in extreme pain. As it was still trying to get to its feet, Danny jumped on its back, and ran across it like it was a small, bony hill. When he reached the neck, he put his knife to work. It wasn't the easiest thing to use, but it was all he had.

Danny reached around and cut into the underside of the neck. Green blood sprayed onto him, and using the knife was like trying to cut through a log with scissors. The Ebulba started to cry out once again, until Danny hit its vocal chords. It tried to raise up again on its back legs, but didn't have the strength. Danny kept cutting, getting more and more of the green blood on him. It had soaked his jacket, and was running down his face into his eyes. He could barely see what he was doing. The creature's front legs were too short to reach behind it, so it began swinging its tail wildly, hoping to hit its attacker. Danny did his best to avoid the spikes, but he was barely hanging on the way it was. He had no idea how much he had left to cut, but thought he had to be nearly through.

Loki ran back down the ramp just as Danny was finishing cutting through the last strands of bone and sinew. As his knife finally came free, the Ebulba's head fell off in front of it. The body collapsed on top of the head, sending Danny rolling off and onto the hard ground, where he lay panting for a moment. As soon as his strength began returning, he simply pointed at the neck stump of the creature. Loki ran over and began dumping salt onto it. The neck sizzled when the salt hit, sending out puffs of green smoke.

When Danny was finally able to find his feet, he stood and looked down at himself. There was very little that wasn't covered in the green, slime-like blood. He ran his hands through his hair, flipping it out of his face. He sighed and walked over to Loki, took the can of gas, and began pouring it on the body.

"Are you supposed to burn it?" Loki asked.

"I have no idea," Danny said. He was exhausted and panting. "I'm just not taking any chances."

He finished pouring the gas, reached into his pocket and found a book of matches. Loki looked at the matches questioningly, but Danny just shrugged. He was too tired to use any magic. He lit the match and threw it on the body, sending flames up into the sky.

The two stood looking at the burning body for a moment in silence. Finally, Loki asked, "What are we going to do with the body?"

"Leave it for the owner. It's their problem to deal with," Danny said. He turned and started walking for the ramp. He wanted to get home and get a shower more than anything in the world right now. He stopped, yelling over his shoulder. "And Loki? When we get some free time, you're learning Latin. You've had hundreds of years to do it. I'm not going to let you keep putting it off."

5

In which Danny and Loki meet a new ally and check out an antiques collection.

Danny got a message from Liz later that day. The meeting was set, that night, at a little gallery her boyfriend owned.

Danny and Loki drove over to 1st Street, looking for the place. Neither spoke, Danny out of sheer excitement, Loki out of nerves. Everything seemed to be lining up a little too perfectly.

The gallery itself wasn't exactly what you'd call a real gallery. It was an old house, nestled among other homes just off of 1st. It stood out among the rest though, as it was the only Victorian house on the whole street. Two white 9's hung beside the door, the other numbers having fallen off long ago. Large windows gazed out into Austin, and Danny could imagine someone standing just to the side of one of those windows, watching them.

Liz answered the door before Danny could even knock. "Glad you could make it," she said. Danny nodded. "He's excited about this." She paused, cocking her head a bit. "I'm not sure why, though. There's something pretty damn special about these things, isn't there?"

"You could say that," Loki answered.

Liz let her gaze drop to him, noticing the

imp for the first. She smiled widely at him. "I didn't realize Danny was bringing a friend. I'm Liz. It's very nice to meet you."

She put out her hand for Loki to shake it, but instead, he turned over her hand and kissed it. "Loki Bartholomew Jones," he said. "Danny's told me all about you, but he failed to mention how beautiful you were."

Liz blushed at this, her face turning almost as red as her hair. "I'm sure he's had a lot on his mind," she answered, "what with monster attacks and all that."

Loki managed to hide his surprise. "You have no idea, madame," he simply stated.

Danny interrupted, before Loki could say anymore. "So, are we-"

"Yes, sorry," Liz answered. "Follow me."

She lead them into the house, which for the most part seemed to be a normal home, except that Danny noticed all the furniture and furnishings were incredibly old. It made *him* feel a bit old, remembering when all these now 'antiques' were all the rage. Gothic paintings hung on almost every free space on the wall. Books filled shelves to the point of almost overflowing. Thick rugs of deep red ran the length of the floors. Danny could get happily lost in a place like this.

Liz lead them to a set of steps leading down into a basement. From his experience, Danny was expecting a dark, dank, dirt room, but instead found a very modern basement, with heavy concrete lining the walls and track lighting casting light into the darkest corners. Like the upstairs, this too was filled with memories of years gone by, although all the artifacts in the basement were on metal shelving, five rows running across the basement. These antiques looked to be much older. Down here were stone tablets, ancient sculptures, and what looked to Danny to be a replica of the Ark of the Covenant. And standing at the end of one of the rows was a young man.

"Guys," Liz said, stopping beside the man, "this is my boyfriend, Jason Wyndham."

The young man turned around, and Daniel was a bit caught off guard. Here he was, surrounded by the ancient and the old, even Liz herself had an old beauty to her, and yet, this man seemed so... modern. He had short-cropped dark hair, a short black beard, neatly trimmed, and the type of glasses that made Danny think of those people that didn't really need them, but wore them to be trendy. He was dressed simply, a Modoc t-shirt and beat up jeans. Everything about him just seemed wrong to Danny. This couldn't be the guy who had the stones.

Jason stuck out his hand. "It's a pleasure to finally meet you," he said. Danny hesitantly shook the hand. "Lizzy has been telling me all about the excitement you two had the other night."

"Just a typical weekend really," Danny shrugged.

Jason studied him for a moment, then shook his head. "You don't like to mess around," he said. "I can tell. So I guess we should get down to business. Follow me."

Jason took the papers that he had been studying, and placed them into a metal box on the closest shelf. From what Danny could see, one was written on paper in German, dated 1943. The other looked to be written on papyrus and was ancient Hebrew. Both carried a lightning bolt and the Death's head symbol at the top. A third looked to be a blueprint of a building Danny was familiar with, but he couldn't seem to place it. He just knew it was something he should know.

Once the papers were locked up, Jason lead them down an aisle, talking the whole way. "I was surprised when Lizzy told me you were trying to track down the stones. So few people have ever even heard of them, it's always a bit shocking to actually meet someone else in the know. I've spent my whole life tracking down ancient oddities." He gestured at the shelves. "Most of this stuff wouldn't even be considered worth anything to actual antique dealers. But I get the feeling that sort of thing doesn't mean much to you." Jason stopped at the end of the row. A large safe was built into this wall, large enough to walk in. It had both a combination lock and an electronic keypad. Danny was glad to see that at least the guy had the good sense to take care of the stones.

"Am I right about you so far, Daniel?" Jason asked.

"Please, just Danny. And so far, I'd say you're right."

"Which means you're not interested in the monetary value. And you're after the stones for... other reasons," Jason said. He was watching Danny closely, possibly hoping that Danny might give away the true reason he was here.

Liz gave a small laugh, just enough to break the tension. "Jason is big into collecting old occult artifacts. Vases supposedly from Atlantis and old diodes that rumor says were used in Nazi experiments." She smiled at Danny. "Don't let him get to you. I told him about the monsters, so now he thinks these stones might have some sort of sinister purpose."

Jason smiled at her, then looked back at Danny and Loki. "I just like to try to read people. What's the point of just collecting all this stuff if you can't figure out the people who used them, or might be wanting to use them."

"It's a good policy to have," Danny said. "Besides, no reason to want to accidentally deal with crazy people."

This brought out a laugh in Jason. "Danny, I do believe you're a man after my own heart." He turned to Liz. "We're being awfully rude to our guests," he said. "Could you do me a huge favor?" Liz nodded. "Okay, there's a bottle of brandy and some glasses in the library. Could you run up and get them?"

"Sure," Liz said.

"You gentlemen do like brandy?" Jason asked.

"It's my favorite brown liquid," Loki replied.

Liz turned and headed towards the stairs. Jason watched her the whole way. Danny's gaze never left Jason.

Once Liz was on her way up the stairs and out of earshot, Jason turned his attention back to Danny. "We'll have to be quick," he said. "She doesn't know much about the stones and I'd prefer to keep it that way." Danny nodded. Jason glanced down to Loki and then back to Danny. "When she told me about the encounter with the demons, I assumed you were legit. Bringing an imp? That just proves it." He turned and began entering numbers into the keypad, nine in total, and then moved to the combination lock.

"I could just be a midget," Loki offered.

"No, it's okay," Jason said with a laugh. He seemed a bit more at ease now that Liz was out of the room. "I'm glad you at least have an idea of what you're dealing with." He stopped working on the combination and turned to face them once again. "But I have to ask before we go any further. What exactly are you wanting the stones for?"

Danny hesitated for a moment. "Do you know what the stones do?" he asked. "What they truly do, when they're assembled all together?"

"I do," Jason answered. "They can destroy the world, wipe out existence in total."

"Close enough," Danny said.

"They can't destroy existence?" Jason asked.

"They can be used a bit more specifically. Depending on the spell, some things could be left. These only destroy living things. You'd have to try and track down a whole different set of artifacts to actually unmake existence. But that's not really the point."

"No, I guess not. And I must tell you, if that's why you're looking for the stones, I'm afraid our business is done right now." Jason smiled at them, friendly, but Danny knew there was an edge to it. It gave Danny a sense of relief.

"No, that's the last thing we want."

The edge dropped out of Jason's body. "So I'm guessing you're trying to gather them to destroy them."

"You would be correct," Danny said.

"And good riddance to the damn things," Loki said. "We've had enough troubles over the years without these things floating around out there."

"Agreed," Jason said. He resumed working on the combination. "These are far too dangerous to be left to the wrong people."

"So why are you collecting them?" Danny asked.

"The same reason as you," Jason said, finishing up the lock and turning the handle on the safe. The door cracked open. Jason nodded to Danny and Loki, telling them that Liz was back.

Liz set the tray of brandy and glasses on a nearby shelf, and poured each of the men a glass. She passed them out and told Danny, "I hate the stuff."

Jason raised his glass to make a toast. "To the end of the search," he said. Danny and Loki returned the gesture and drank. The brandy was wonderful. They each set their glasses down, and Jason lead them into the safe.

The inside was spacious but almost entirely empty. There was one shelf on each wall, except for the wall surrounding the door and the one opposite it, and on each shelf, four heavy lead boxes. Jason went to each one and opened it, until all eight were exposed. The stones didn't look like much, but Danny was impressed.

Of the nineteen stones, they were split into six families, identified by color, each family originally coming from a different region of the world. The four Sumerian red stones, the four Akkadian blue stones, the four Vedic amber stones, the four Xian emerald stones, the two Atlantean white stones, and the final stone, a jet black Hyperborean stone. Unfortunately, Danny knew exactly where the Hyperborean stone was.

As to who had created the stones, that remained a mystery. Danny had once asked his former colleagues, who were usually in the know about that sort of thing, but none of them had any answers. The best he could get was, "Whoever created them did so in the complete and utter darkness." Danny had no idea what that meant.

Danny looked at each one carefully, silently. All four of the red stones, three blues, and a white. The white stone particularly impressed him, as it was considered to be one of the hardest to find. Danny himself had the other one, and had spent a considerable amount of time searching for this one. He had almost convinced himself it wasn't on the Earth realm anymore, and yet, here it sat.

Jason noticed Danny eying that one and said, "Bought it from a man looking to get rid of it in a hurry. I think he needed the money pretty desperately. Met the guy in a market." He gave Danny a knowing look. Danny was more intrigued with Jason with each passing moment.

Loki pulled out a small tuning fork and began moving to each stone, putting the fork against each, his ear close to the fork. With each stone, he gave a satisfied grunt. After he had finished with the last stone, he told Danny, "They're real. Every single one of them."

"I guess we should discuss price," Danny said to Jason, but Jason simply waved him off.

"No need to," he said. "It sounds like we both have the same end goal in mind for the stones. And Lizzy tells me you have the other eleven?"

"No, I have ten," Danny admitted. He looked at Loki. "We're scheduled to get the last one later this week."

"That's good enough for me," Jason said. "As long as you'll let me help in the... showing of the stones," he looked at Liz to make sure she hadn't picked up on his subtle hint and continued, "I have no problem combining our two collections to the benefit of all of us."

"That is absolutely agreeable," Danny said. "You have no idea how great this is."

Jason smiled. "The feeling is mutual, Daniel. Now, how about another drink to celebrate?"

The Book of Daniel

Interlude
France, 1702

The crowded town square had taken on a smell, one that was particularly rotten, and not just because of the day's events. The smell was a mixture of the unbathed with an underlying scent of fear. The population of this town was watching the devil's work.

Or at least, that's what their town and spiritual leader, Reverend Guy Lumios told them. This was the devil's work, and he intended to set it right. They, as members of this community, must watch and see that nothing so evil ever came to pass again.

Lumios stood on a large wooden platform at one end of the square, directly in front of the church. As the square now seemed to be full, and the clock was striking noon, he began the proceedings.

"I will make this quick, for justice must be enacted swiftly," Lumios told the crowd, his voice loud and booming out to them. It was the voice of a man who has a talent for these sort of things, a man who used his instrument properly. "There has been evil present in our beautiful hamlet, and that evil must be stomped out. We believed we had erased this evil, all those many years ago, but we were incorrect. There was still one source of evil."

At this, two large men dressed in executioner's black lead out the damned. She was a petite woman, beautiful auburn hair, sparkling green eyes. She was dressed in a plain, dull smock, the clothing of a peasant. Her hands were bound behind her back. And she was scared. Her eyes clearly showed her fear. She searched the faces of the nearby crowd, seeking someone, anyone, who might come to her rescue. All she found was hate and anger.

The two men lead her across the platform, to another raised platform. They lead her up the few steps, and stopped at the top. Lumios nodded at them. They placed the hanging noose over her head and tightened it around her neck. Once finished, they stepped off the higher platform in unison, taking up a place on each side of it.

Reverend Lumios continued. "Jean-Marie Islington, nee Clobert, you have been accused and convicted on the crime of witchcraft. As such, you have been sentenced to be hanged until there is no more life in your body. You have corrupted this village. May God in all his gloriousness have mercy on your vile, black soul."

"Wait," Jean-Marie screamed, using every ounce of energy she had to stave off her death. "I have had no trial! I have had no chance to defend myself!" Once again, she desperately searched the crowd, hoping for some sign of help, of mercy. This time, at least, her gaze found some that had a look of questioning, of confusion on their faces.

"You have not the reason nor the right to defend yourself," Reverend Lumios said. "This

office has found, by records of your own record-
ing, that you, at present, are the age of seventy,
and yet, you look not a day over twenty. Tell me,
mademoiselle, how, but witchcraft, could you
explain such a thing?"

Lumios waited patiently, as if honestly hoping for a reasonable answer.

"I have no explanation," Jean-Marie admitted. An angry murmuring spread the crowd. The
faces showing questioning turned once more to
anger and fear. "But this was not by my own doing," she said defiantly. "I have never practiced
witchcraft or the occult in my life. I am a good
servant in the name of God."

"God does not grant one life beyond one's
own mortal boundaries," Lumios told the accused. He stepped to the edge of the platform
and placed his hand on the lever that would
drop the bottom out from her platform.

"It must have been my husband!" Jean-
Marie shouted. "I have done nothing. If there
was witchcraft afoot, it must have been him."

Lumios nodded, as if expecting that. "Yes,
your husband. A man none in this village have
met, nor seen. Tell us, please, where is your husband? If he is here, let him stand before us to
give proper explanation to these events."

Jean-Marie waited. No one spoke up.

"I do not know where he is," she said, hope
leaving her voice as she spoke. "He comes and
goes. I have not seen him for weeks."

"Then again I say, may God have mercy on
your soul." Lumios pulled the lever. The bottom
dropped from the platform, the rope tightening.

Jean-Marie hung, no cloth about her face to hide her death visage from the crowd. The fall was not steep enough to snap her neck. Instead, she hung, suffocating. Her eyes began to bulge, seeming almost to leave her skull. Her mouth twisted, foaming. Her body danced and jigged, bouncing, trying to find a position to ease the pulling on her neck. Horrible grunts left her body as her face grew redder.

"See, now, all those who look upon this scene!" cried Reverend Lumios. "See the true face of evil. It was this evil that has beset upon our crops, causing none to grow. It was this evil that has dried up our wells. It is this evil that has caused nightmares among our children. See this face of evil. Now see it perish!"

Jean-Marie's body gave one last jolt, and then stopped moving. The face, which had turned a beet red, began to fade into a pale, deathly white. Jean-Marie Islington was dead.

Deep among the crowd, a beautiful man stood, watching the proceedings. Dark hair, dark, haunting eyes, tall and muscular, he looked like a beauty only God could craft. He stood watching, tears in his eyes.

He did not notice the small man that had come to stand by his side. It was the smell of smoke that alerted him to his presence. He turned, and there stood a hairy man, half the size of a normal human, smoking a cigar. The small man looked at him.

"Nothing like a hanging to put the fear into people, is there?" the small man said. He gave a wicked smile as he said it.

"I find your comment to be in poor taste," the beautiful man said.

"Odd that it would be found in poor taste," the smaller man said. The crowd was beginning to break up and move their separate ways, but the beautiful man continued staring at the hanging woman. "Unless, of course, you were someone close to the dearly departed. Then you might find my comment offensive." The little man gave his sick smile again.

The beautiful man turned on him, anger in his eyes. "And if this crowd knew what you were, imp, you would be hanging in her place next," he said. A few in the passing crowd caught the anger in the voice, but none could hear the words clearly, so they continued walking.

The imp simply nodded. "And what if they knew of you?" he asked. "What do you think they would do? Hang you? Or perhaps praise you?" The beautiful man looked at him, contemplating what to do. "I know what you are," the imp said, "but this isn't the place for that discussion. Now, Daniel, why don't we go have a drink? I hear the wine in this particular region is quite good." The imp began to walk away, but turned to look back at Daniel. "Name's Loki, by the way. Now, come along. You and I have business to discuss."

Loki the imp ordered a bottle of wine for himself. Daniel simply wanted a mug of ale. After the barmaid delivered their drinks, Loki poured himself a glass and sat back to examine Daniel. "So," he asked, sipping on his wine, "what do you think of all the goings on?"

Daniel looked at him, stone-faced. "What do you mean?"

"The war, the succession, all that. France has become very interesting as of late," the imp asked.

"I care not for public matters."

"Not a very talkative one, are you?"

"My wife has just been hung for crimes she did not commit. At the moment, the affairs of humanity hold little interest for me." Daniel took a long pull from his ale. He used the back of his sleeve to wipe foam from his mouth. Loki continued studying him.

"I think you care quite a bit, actually," he said.

Daniel's face betrayed him, if only for a moment. "I do not. Whatever feelings I might have had, died on those gallows with my wife."

"If you don't care, why didn't you speak up at the proceedings?"

"They would have murdered her either way," he answered simply. Daniel had thought about this for days, agonizing over it, and decided it was true.

"The good Reverend is not as good as he appears," Loki said, finishing his wine and pouring another glass.

"No, he is not," Daniel agreed.

"You could have presented yourself, shown them who and what you are. You could have told these people what type of person he truly is."

"I could have. But it is not my place to judge. It is their place to find out the truth. Seeking the truth, finding a deeper understanding, is one of the points of humanity."

Loki nodded. "As is the eternal cycle of life and death." Daniel stared at him. "You know this to be true. Even if you had spoke up, she would have died eventually. Your wives don't live forever, do they?"

"No," Daniel admitted. "They do not. It was no way to die, though."

"Your guilt still shines through," Loki said. Daniel cast his eyes down, staring into his mug. "Perhaps that is why you let this happen. Guilt over humanity's flaws. Guilt that death would find her eventually. Guilt that you made the wrong choice coming here to begin with."

Daniel drained the mug and looked at the imp. "What do you want?"

"There's the anger, the passion I was looking for," the imp said.

"You seem to know quite a bit about me, little one."

"I have been watching you. I always watch those I intend to work with," Loki said with a wave of his hand. "Besides, we have met before."

"Have we?"

"Prague. Almost a year ago."

The barmaid came and refilled Daniel's mug. He had not intended to drink more, but he was beginning to find himself intrigued with this conversation. He waited until the barmaid was gone.

"That vampire clan? That was a bad bit of business," he said. "But I don't remember you there."

"I wasn't fighting at the time, simply a bystander trapped in that damn town hall, waiting for a savior."

Daniel nodded. "Was my work deemed satisfactory?"

"Oh, the vampires did not bother the town again," Loki said. "That is not to say you took care of them all."

"There are more?"

"Yes, in this very town. They have been hunting you for quite some time now. Seeking revenge for killing their offspring."

"The elders were not there," Daniel said, more to himself than the imp. "That explains why they seemed so disorganized." He nodded to the imp. "I thank you for the warning."

"I am not here simply to give you information. I am also here asking for help."

"I told you, I am not interested in the affairs of others right now."

"Yes, you told me that, and as I pointed out, you are lying," Loki said. "Besides, I think you will find this mission intriguing."

"Why do you believe that?"

"It concerns a coven of witches in Russia."

Daniel made a face of disgust. "I've had my fill of cries of witchcraft. I want nothing to do with any of it."

"Oh, but these are true witches," Loki responded.

"Then let the proper authorities handle them. I wish to keep to myself for the time being. If the vampires come for me, I will deal with them, but otherwise, I only wish to stay out of society for a while."

"It is understandable," Loki agreed. "But tell

me, Daniel, have you ever heard of the Terrarum Exstinctor stones?"

Daniel froze, his mug halfway between the table and his mouth. "Of course I have," he said. "I know very little of them, but I have heard of them. What of it?"

"There's a coven of witches in possession of some of these stones, and that could be very bad for a lot of people," Loki said.

"I have heard that they can increase the magical power a person can wield. I would think any good witchfinder could deal with that."

"Oh, Danny, my boy," Loki said, that wicked grin appearing on his face again. "You have no idea just how dangerous these things can be. Just think of the name." Daniel thought for a moment, and nodded. "This is the sort of thing people like you and I were made for."

"Are they truly world destroyers?" Daniel asked.

Loki's grin grew larger. He knew right then, no matter how upset Daniel might be with humanity, he would never, ever turn his back on them. And that is exactly what the world needed.

The Reverend Guy Lumios walked out of the little house that sat in an alley, checking both ways to make sure he was not seen. Confident that there was no one around, he stepped onto the street and began the walk back to his church. In his head, he was already composing his next sermon, something rousing, to make the people of this village forget all about the awful events of this day. So lost in his thoughts was he, that he never noticed the shadows growing and moving in the street, not until he heard the voices.

"He wears the stink of our enemy," the first voice said, a deep, guttural voice.

"Yes, but he, too, is an enemy of our enemy," the second answered, as horrible as the first.

Lumios stopped and looked around, trying to discern if the voices were talking to him. For the first time, he noticed just how dark it was.

"And he is a man of the cloth," the first voice said.

The second voice gave a laugh, a horrible, black laugh. "Perhaps we should have some fun," it said.

"Yes, and we are so, so hungry," the first answered.

Reverend Lumios noticed, too late, the moving shadows, darker and blacker than any night he had ever seen. The darkness fell over him. And the darkness had such sharp teeth.

6

In which Danny and Loki take an interstellar journey, many explanations are offered, horrors are seen, and Loki prepares for the worst.

Danny awoke with a start. It was dawn, and the sun was just creeping above the horizon. He got out of bed and made his way silently to the kitchen. From just outside the door, he could see Loki sitting at the little round kitchen table, nervous and fidgety.

Today was the day they went to Hell.

Danny had not yet entered the kitchen, not even made a sound, but Loki knew he was there. "I've made a list of all the supplies we'll need," the imp said.

"We already got all of our supplies last week," Danny answered. He walked into the kitchen and poured himself coffee. "I don't think I've ever seen you up this early."

Loki ignored this last bit. "We got the supplies needed to open the doorway. But you didn't tell me that the amulet wasn't working."

Danny shrugged and sat down next to Loki. "It was a bit strange. The amulet should have hidden my location from anyone seeking me out. But I didn't think it was enough to worry you about."

"Yeah, just what I want. Living in the same apartment with a guy who's being hunted by demons," Loki finished his coffee and sat staring at the empty cup.

"They were just delivering me a message. They wanted me to stay out of Hell."

"All the more reason to go get some extra protection." Loki picked up a copy of the newspaper from the table. "Have you seen this?" he asked.

Danny quickly scanned the paper. He could easily pick out the article Loki was talking about. Someone was on a killing spree through the southwest. Authorities thought they were headed to Vegas.

Danny tossed the paper back onto the table. "Sounds bad," he said. Loki nodded. "But nothing we can take care of right now."

"You know just as well as I do what's behind those killings."

"Sounds like a vampire," Danny said. "Probably at least a couple, from the sound of it."

"And?" Loki asked.

"And what?" Danny responded. "We have other matters to attend to. What is it you want me to do?"

"Call off our trip to Hell and take care of this. Vampires are bad news and you know it."

"We're not calling off the trip. You don't have to go," Danny added. He was a little annoyed. Probably lack of sleep on top of the bad dream he just had, he thought.

"I'm going," Loki said. "I'm not letting you go on your own anymore. Too dangerous."

"Okay, then we go get the stone. There's plenty of occult hunters out there. I'm sure one of them can handle this," Danny said. Loki rolled his eyes.

"Hey," Danny said, his agitation showing through, "Tracking down the stones were your idea in the first place."

"I know," Loki sighed again. "I guess I'm just getting paranoid."

"Trips to Hell can do that."

"It's not just that." Loki stood up and went to refill his cup. "It's everything. A guy pops into your life with all of the missing stones. You get a vision that you need to save a girl who happens to be his girlfriend. Your protection amulet stops working just long enough for demons to deliver a message." He finished filling his cup and turned back to Danny. "There's a lot of coincidences all of a sudden. Almost makes me wonder if something bigger isn't at work here. I'm just starting to feel like maybe we shouldn't be messing with the stones right now."

"You want to just give up?" Danny asked.

"Of course not. The stones are far too dangerous to be left alone out there." The imp sat back down at the table, and put his hand on Danny's arm. "I'm just asking you to think about this. Forces seem to be mounting against us. Maybe we should just let things cool off for a bit. I mean, we know where all the other stones are now."

"Even more reason to finish it," Danny said. He'd always had a bit of a rebellious streak, and the thought of Loki of all people telling him not to worry about the stones brought it out of him. He really didn't enjoy taking orders. "I'd feel a lot safer if they were destroyed as quickly as possible."

"Fair enough," the imp said, finally giving in. "So the market, then Hell?"

"Not quite," Danny said. "I was thinking breakfast first. Time moves differently when it comes to the other realms. We have no idea when we might get to eat again."

"No food in Hell, I'm guessing."

"Oh, you could find food," Danny said, "but you don't want to eat it. That leads to nothing but trouble."

Loki laughed. He seemed to be cheering up a bit, even though Danny could tell he was still troubled.

"We'll do the market after we get back from Hell," Danny said, finishing his coffee and heading to his room to change clothes.

"Hold on, why are we waiting?" Loki asked.

"Well, we have all the supplies to open the portal. The amulet won't actually work in Hell. Protective charms don't work. Neither do healing spells," Danny shrugged. "One of Lucifer's little rules, I guess. Besides, once we get the stone and get back, we'll have to go pick up the other stones I have so we can destroy them."

"But why would we go to..." Loki trailed off, realizing where Danny had been hiding the stones. "Zed's? They've been hidden away at Zed's?"

Danny nodded. "I thought it was the safest place. I hated having them out of my sight, but thought being with me wasn't a great idea either. Besides, in those early days, we were barely able to carry enough supplies for the two of us, let alone a bunch of magical stones."

Loki hung his head, an angry look in his eyes. "You should have told me you'd hidden them there."

"I know," Danny said, softly, sounding a bit sorry, even though he felt no reason to. "But... do you remember Venezuela?" Loki nodded, anger immediately leaving his face. "Those thugs tortured you. And I got afraid. I thought it would be better if I was the only person who knew where the stones were."

"Okay. But Zed? You weren't worried about him? Someone has already done a number on him. Aren't you afraid he'll tell somebody."

"Oh, Zed doesn't know what he has," Danny laughed. "All he's ever seen is some old weapons and paperwork. He thinks I'm trying to hide my valuables with him. Have a little faith in me."

Loki gave a fake bow. "I bow before the king of lies."

Danny went into his room and started changing into what he felt were his battle clothes. Plain white t-shirt, jeans, black boots, and a light leather jacket. He turned to find Loki watching him.

"There is one other thing," Loki said.

"I figured," Danny said, dropping his typical supplies into his jacket pockets. Simple things, nothing overly extravagant. Darkness powder, sage, a silver cross, wooden stake, and a small flashlight. Nothing else seemed very useful in

Hell.

"Will we have to meet them?" Loki asked.

Danny showed concern over his little friend's question. "If we're lucky, we'll completely avoid them. But if not, they're really not that bad. You just have to be careful of them."

"They're not that bad?"

"Okay, well they're not exactly good," Danny laughed. "They're kind of like a used car salesman, only a lot smoother. You just know everything you might get from them has a price. So, just don't take anything from them, and you'll be fine." Finished with gathering his supplies, Danny knelt down and put his hands on Loki's shoulders. "One more thing, and this is extremely important. Avoid staring into their eyes as much as you can. They can be hypnotizing. They'll try and draw you in to their spell and find out your true name."

"No problem there," Loki said. "As far as I know, it's just Loki. I'll gladly tell them that."

"No," Danny shook his head. "It's kind of hard to explain, but everyone has what is considered their true name. It's what makes up their entire person, both who and what they are. And if someone learns that name, they have power over that person."

"But I don't know my true name, I guess."

"Doesn't matter. Your soul knows it, deep down. Most people are never conscious of their true name, but it can be pulled out of them. I've never met a human that can do it, and there are very few creatures that can find out someone's true name. Lucifer is one of the few things in existence that can." Danny patted him on the shoulders.

Loki nodded. "Just out of curiosity, do you know yours?"

"I do," Danny answered. "But no one can get mine. I've hidden it away. Long story for another time."

Loki nodded once more, but he still looked apprehensive. Danny gave him a smile.

"Don't worry. Everything will be fine," Danny said, starting for the door. He was ready to grab a decent meal and get on with it. "You'll be with me, and I know how to handle them. Like I said, they're not that bad. I like to call them Lucy." Danny laughed. "Come on, let's go get breakfast.

The pair grabbed breakfast at Baby Acapulco's, as many breakfast tacos as they could eat, even though Loki didn't seem to have much of an appetite. Danny couldn't really blame him. It was nerve-wracking, taking a trip into Hell. They headed back to the apartment, driving slowly, the convertible top down, music up. Danny wanted to take his time and relax. The late spring sun streamed down over Austin, washing the city in color. These moments were what Danny lived for, what he fought for.

Once back at the apartment, there was little discussion. Both Danny and Loki knew what needed to be done, and both knew their parts well. Loki began drawing the chalk circle on the floor of their spare bedroom, while Danny began mixing the herbs they would need. As Loki began to add the markings that would open the doorway to Hell as opposed to one of the other realms, Danny set fire to the mixed herbs. Loki nodded at Danny as he was finished. Both stepped inside the circle.

"You don't need a book or something for the incantation?" Loki asked.

Danny shook his head. "Got it memorized."

"Good," Loki said. "Don't know how anyone can read Latin, let alone memorize it, but that's one less thing to carry."

Danny took the ashes from the bowl in one hand, and took Loki's hand with his other. "I don't want us to get separated when we're pulled through the door," he said. "It can be a rough ride."

Loki nodded, looking slightly ill. Danny began speaking the incantation. "Lanuam mundi aperi nobis. Nusquam regna aperi nobis." He threw down the ashes, and, his voicing raising to a yell, shouted, "Ad inferos nos audere!"

It felt like the world had opened up underneath them. There was a sensation of falling, quickly and suddenly. Danny felt his stomach drop. It always caught him off guard, no matter how many times he had done it.

There was nothing visible around them, only darkness. Out of nowhere, the world exploded into color. Masses of stars, glowing, pulsing beacons surrounded them. Galaxies, thousands upon thousands, filled their vision. It was an infinite beauty. Danny had heard tell that you could go mad in this space between realms if you failed to set a specific course during the spell. He could understand why. This sort of cosmic vision was enough to overwhelm any man's mind.

Their falling stopped, and, as if a destructive wind had picked up, they were pushed to one side. Danny turned, pulling Loki with him, to face the spot they were being pushed towards. Their path stood out from the rest of the landscape. It looked like what a man can only imagine a black hole must look like, a gaping hole of nothingness cut into a brightly lit cloth. As they approached it, the light began to fade, slowly at first, then rapidly as they got closer. Within the blink of an eye, they were surrounded by darkness again. And then an explosion of light, just as the sensation of moving stopped. They had arrived in Hell.

Danny found himself staring into a soft, springy, green grass. He put his hands onto the ground and pushed up, feeling the wet earth push back against him. He pushed himself into a kneeling position and looked around.

Beside him, Loki was standing up, looking around like Danny. He seemed to be confused.

"Did we screw it up somehow?" the imp asked. He gestured at the scene around them. They were on a grass covered hill. The sun was out, the sky was blue, the air was rich and clean. It was a beautiful, perfect day.

"No," Danny said, getting to his feet. "We're definitely here."

"This can't be right. Hell isn't supposed to look like... like... I don't know, Scotland?"

"Scotland," Danny said, nodding. That was a fairly accurate description. "Like I said, the kinds of tortures you'll see down here aren't what you'd expect. Welcome to Hell, buddy."

Danny set off down the hill with Loki close behind, gazing around him constantly. Hell was *never* quite what you expected.

"I'm not sure I really understand what I'm seeing," Loki said, panting a bit trying to keep up with Danny.

"That's why I didn't try explaining it fully before," Danny answered. "It's something you have to see. Even then, it's still hard to understand."

"So, Hell is grass and hills and blue skies? Cause that doesn't sound too bad."

"I'd say some people would argue that with you. And that's kind of the point." Danny stopped for a moment to let Loki catch his breath. The hill seemed to stretch on forever. "Hell is what could be considered an abstract."

Loki simply looked at him. "Yeah, Danny, I have no idea what that means."

"Hell is constantly changing. It depends on the souls that are trapped here. It's not all lakes of fire and that sort of thing, although you can find that here. Each individual makes their own impression of Hell, and that impression becomes reality."

"Okay, I guess I kind of get that," Loki answered, bent over, hands on his knees.

"Basically, all Lucifer does is oversee the place. It's the souls that are trapped here that create the horrific nature of the place," Danny said. "Each person who is here is here because their guilt and their sins brought them. That's not to say the people aren't guilty. I mean, of course serial killers and child molesters and all of that are here. But the majority of the people? They're here because they believe this is what they deserve. They are sinners, and good people do get in to Heaven, but the people down here have committed just enough sin so that they're not really good enough for Heaven, and just guilty enough to believe they should be in Hell. So they create their own devices of torture to give them exactly what they feel they deserve. Humans are far more creative than demons or angels. They end up punishing themselves in ways only they can imagine."

"Makes sense," Loki said, finally straightening up. "So who's Hell are we in right now?"

"Mine." Danny started walking again. Loki stared at him for a moment in shock and then ran to catch up.

"You want to say that again. I think I must have misheard you," the imp said.

"You heard just fine. This is my Hell," Danny said, not looking back.

"Well, you certainly have an interesting idea of punishment."

"It's a long story," Danny said.

"Aren't they all?" The imp walked silently, thinking to himself. "So, how do you find anything down here?" he finally asked.

"How do you mean?"

"If Hell is constantly changing, how do you know where anything is? Wouldn't things be moving all the time?"

"Ah," Danny said. "Yeah, some things do move, but only in this area. The place we're in right now, it's called the Ethereal Plains. This is where the majority of the souls are."

"Are they here right now?"

"Yeah, they're all around us. We just can't see them and they can't see us. All of them are too busy, too involved, wrapped up in their own punishments." Danny stopped for a moment. In the distance at the bottom of the hill, something was just starting to come into view.

"So why can I see you?"

Danny turned to look at Loki, shaken out of his distraction. "You're a magical creature, not human. Because of that, you don't create an impression on Hell. Plus, when I took your hand in the apartment, that bound us together on the trip. So you're seeing what I see."

"But aren't you-" Loki started to ask, but Danny cut him off.

"I have magical abilities, and I'm not quite human, but Hell still affects me." Danny started walking again, heading for the landmark that was coming into view.

"Okay," Loki started, clearly trying to think of how he wanted to proceed. "So we're in the Ethereal Plains now. I'm guessing there are other places in Hell?"

"Yeah. Think of Hell like an apple. The Ethereal Plains are the outer part, the part you eat."

"And the core?" Loki asked.

"That's the Pit," Danny answered.

"And what exactly will we find in the Pit?"

The closer they got, the more features they were able to see of what they were approaching. Danny could now see that it was a small house, not much more than a shack really. Smoke was coming out of a broken stone chimney. He kept walking.

"The Pit is where all the stuff you normally hear about Hell is," he said. "That's where the demons live, that's where it's dark and hot, Lucifer's castle is there, the lake of fire, which we'll hopefully avoid. All that stuff."

"The lake of fire really that bad?"

"No, just kind of depressing."

Loki nodded, trying to think of any other questions he could ask. He thought of one more. "Why is it called the Pit?"

Danny laughed. "I've never been able to figure that out. I mean, there *is* an actual pit. But it's such a small part of that area, I never understood why they chose to call the whole place the Pit." He shrugged. "Probably not Lucifer's idea. I've always assumed it came from upper management."

"Upper management?"

"The group upstairs, so to speak."

"You don't talk about them often," Loki said softly.

Danny lowered his head, trying to think how to answer that. "I try to stay out of their way," he finally said. "They stay out of mine. Mostly."

"Except for a few days ago," Loki said. "And God? You mentioned you thought he would want the stones destroyed."

"I'm not really sure how much interaction

God has with the angels anymore. He used to be heavily involved with each angel personally. But I just don't know nowadays. I got the impression from Michael that God may not be as involved as he used to be." He frowned at this thought, then shrugged. "But I guess that's his choice. You know, being God and all."

Loki seemed almost as troubled by Danny at this thought. He could think of nothing more to say, so the two walked in silence. Danny wasn't sure how long they walked that way, neither saying a word. It felt like forever, but then again, that might just have been Hell. Time did pass differently here, but it also felt different. A moment could feel like eternity, all depending on how much torture the mind and soul believed it deserved. Because of this, Danny tried to keep his thoughts clear and focused on finding the last stone, which is never easy when there's so many other things trying to force their way into his mind, like the scene they were now finding themselves rapidly approaching.

Danny had of course seen this place before on previous trips. It didn't mean he liked seeing it though. They were close enough now to begin making out the features of the place. It was an old stone house, large enough for only two rooms. The smoke from the chimney grayed out the beautiful day behind it. It was surrounded by an ancient wooden fence, and inside the fence, animals lazily grazed. Mostly sheep and goats, a handful of chickens, but a few cattle as well, standing close to the other building inside the fence, a small wooden barn, the wood panels starting to show their age. But there was something else inside the fence as well. A woman, no more than twenty-five, was feeding the chickens from a bucket. She had long blond hair, and she was beautiful by anyone's standards. She stopped feeding the chickens long enough to look up, in their direction, and scan the horizon.

Danny stopped as she looked, and Loki stopped beside him. The woman continued looking, but finally gave up and went back to feeding the chickens.

"I thought we couldn't see anyone else," Loki said.

"We can see her. She can't see us," Danny answered.

"And how is that possible?"

"It's a bit hard to explain," Danny said, letting out a sigh. "Sometimes, in extremely rare circumstances, some people can share a Hell. She and I share this one."

"You both hate sunny days and pretty hills?"

"No, this is a bad place for both of us," Danny said.

"Why?" Loki asked.

"Because we were both happy here," Danny answered. He stared at the woman, and an intense sorrow filled his face.

"Who is she, Danny?"

"My wife," he said. "Annabel, my last wife." He began walking again.

"I would have thought all your wives made it into Heaven," Loki said.

"They did. Except for this one." Danny stopped at the fence row and stood watching her as she finished feeding the chickens and moved to the barn. At the side of the barn was a pile of wood, which she began gathering into a wheelbarrow.

Loki stood alongside him, ignoring the scene in front of him and instead concentrating on his friend.

"Why did she get stuck down here?" he asked.

Danny continued watching her, but finally answered. "Most of my wives died violently, always due to my life. Whether it was demons or other humans who thought they must be evil, they were almost always killed before their times."

"And this one wasn't."

"No, she died a natural death. She was almost one hundred and seventy years old. The last few times I saw her, she hated me. After a certain point, the eternal youth that seems to strike my partners fades. They age rapidly. Those last few years were hard on her," Danny said. He sighed again, losing himself in the memories. "She became angry and bitter, towards me especially. She wanted nothing more to do with me, so I went away. And a few years later, on her deathbed, she cursed God and all his works for creating a monster like me. So she ended up here."

"That doesn't really seem fair," Loki said. "There were things happening to her that she didn't understand. She shouldn't be blamed for getting angry."

"She was very... vehement in her curses,"

Danny said. "She said a lot of things that, once said, couldn't be taken back. And dying with anger in your heart is no way to go. She was never much of a sinner, not until that last day."

"Do you blame God?"

"Of course not," Danny answered. "It wasn't God's fault she ended up like that. It was mine. I put her on the path that lead her to an unnaturally long life. I'm the reason she's here."

The imp put his hand over his friend's. "You're not a monster, Daniel," he said, "and neither is she. Sometimes, things just don't always go according to the plan, I guess."

Danny nodded, trying to not to let his tears show. "We both see this place now," he said. "It was the place we were happiest together. I guess now it's the place we both regret the most." He tried to swallow, but his throat seemed closed. "Could you give me a few minutes, Loki? I just... I need to..."

"Yeah, of course," Loki said. He walked over to the edge of the fence row, leaving Danny to watch his dead wife go about her daily routine, the one that she would be doing for the rest of eternity.

After a few moments, Danny joined Loki at the side of the house. "Come on," he said. "We should get this over with."

Loki started to ask Danny if he wanted to talk about all this, but Danny waved him off before he could. They were maybe fifty yards from the house when Loki felt like he was having ice cold water poured on him. It didn't necessarily hurt, but it wasn't pleasant, more like a wave on discomfort passing over him.

The world changed around him as the feeling passed. Instead of the sunny, green world he had just been standing in, he was now in what he could only think of as Hell, truly and completely. The sky was a dark and sinister red, filled with smoke instead of clouds. The landscape that had once been oddly comforting and inviting was now barren and desolate, twisted black trees and a few large, hulking mountains dominating the vista. Loki didn't even have to ask Danny. He was sure the mountains were made of bones.

There was a path running in front of them, made of ash and soot, black as the blackest night and stomped down to form a hard paste. Danny set off, Loki trailing behind, not wanting to observe their surroundings, but doing so anyway. It was a dark world, light enough to see, but dark all the same.

"Welcome to the Pit," Danny said. "This path will take us to the castle."

"Lucifer's castle?"

"Yeah. It sits towards the center of Hell."

"What's in the actual center?" Loki asked.

"The pit itself. And the dungeons."

"Hell needs dungeons?"

Danny nodded. "There are some things so bad even Hell needs to lock them away."

Loki shuddered at the thought.

Danny didn't like what he was seeing, but he didn't share that with Loki. The imp seemed disturbed already, but Danny had been to Hell enough to know things didn't seem right in the

Pit. Hell was a desolate place, but there should have been some signs of activity and life, so to speak. Instead, their path was completely empty. While it was certainly helpful to their mission, it also felt like a bad omen. The only thought that came to Danny's mind was, 'Hell is empty and the devils are here.'

Danny lead the way down the path, Loki trailing close behind, not wanting to lose his way. The ashen ground crackled under their feet as they walked, neither saying a word, taking everything in. The air smelled heavy of sulfur and what Loki eventually came to realize was burning fat. He shuddered to think where it might be coming from, but got his answer all too soon.

A little hill gradually sloped upward, leading to a bend in the path. As they came around the bend, the first change in landscape they had seen appeared before them. To the side of the path stood six poles. On each pole hung a person. The pole ran through each person's anus and up through their mouths, blood seeping out of both wounds. Each person was on fire, skin burning and peeling, but never disappearing, creating a never-ending cycle of pain. As the ground crunched under their feet, the eyes of the victims rolled around to watch the duo in anguished silence.

Loki gasped and covered his mouth. Danny put a hand on his friend's shoulder and pulled him along faster. "Just remember," Danny said, "they're only going through that because they believe they should."

Loki nodded and tried his best to keep walking without looking.

The landscape continued to change as they ventured further into the Pit. The mountains they had seen earlier grew larger, and for the first time, Loki could make out the vague shape of a castle in the distance. There were sounds now as well, screams echoing across the deathly landscape, unearthly growls and howls, and occasionally what sounded like the beating of a heavy drum.

This was what Danny experienced on every trip to this damned place. It was a miracle that he hadn't lost his mind the first time he made the trip into Hell. As they walked, Danny remembered it. His former employer had made a special request of him to travel here. He had dreaded it immediately. The suffering in this place seeped into everything, twisting and turning it into ugliness. He had cried the first time he saw a human being eaten alive, the demon simply smiling and offering him a bite. By the time he reached the castle, he thought he would just quit, simply go home, and try to never think of Hell again. But Lucifer had taken him in, listened to what must have sounded like insane ramblings, calmed him down, and explained how Hell worked. Danny still didn't like it, but he understood it, and understood its necessity in the universe.

The difference between now and then was that now the horrific landscape seemed emptier than it should have been.

A partial explanation came to Danny when

they approached the first intersection on the path. Loki tugged on his sleeve when it came into sight. Danny nodded and told him, "Keep walking." They continued on. The path split into two forks. The fork on the left, veering off of the main path, was blocked. Standing in the way were two large... creatures was the best Danny could think of to call them. They were well over ten feet tall, covered neck to toe in armor that looked to be one solid piece, a separate helmet atop their bodies, a v-shape opening in the helmet that showed no face behind it. The armor was pitch black, but seemed to have a shimmering quality to it, which always reminded Danny of a starry night. In one hand, each held a six foot pike, the tip blood red, the only color to the creatures. In the other hand, each held a sword, pointed towards the ground, heavy steel surrounded by a ethereal glow. Danny knew these were Hell's version of the angels' fiery swords.

Danny and Loki moved past the hulking, armored forms. They made no motion to show that they knew Danny and Loki were there, but Danny was cautious all the same. Once safely past, Danny breathed a little easier and slowed his walking.

"What were those?" Loki asked.

"Royal Guard of Lucifer," Danny said, pausing to scan the horizon, then walking on. "I was wondering why we hadn't seen anyone. Normally, there's demons out on the path, coming and going around the Pit. For whatever reason, the Guard seems to be keeping everyone off the paths."

"Any idea why?"

"There's a million reasons why Lucifer might be doing that," Danny wrinkled his forehead trying to think. "They didn't seem to pose any threat to us. And they didn't try to stop us. I'm not sure what's going on, but Hell seems to be an interesting place today."

"The swords-" Loki began.

"Demon blades. Angels have swords that can kill almost anything in existence. Lucifer's Guard has swords that can take down almost anything in Hell. Not as good as a fiery sword, but upper management didn't want Lucifer taking out any angels."

"What are they, underneath the armor?"

Danny laughed. "I have no idea. I've never asked, and I don't want to. Just remember, they're the baddest of the bad down here, so try not to piss them off. There's not very many, but if you mess with one, they'll all be on you."

They continued on, shortly passing a four-way intersection. A pair of guards stood at opposite sides of the path, leaving Danny and Loki no choice but to continue going forward. At the sides of the path, small signs of civilization began popping up. Broken tools and weapons, the vague remnants of tracks from wheels in the path, broken trees that looked like they had possibly been shaped to offer shelter, spilled blood.

Danny explained. "On a normal day down here, we would have seen quite a few people by now. Demons as well. I also would have taken us down a different path to avoid running into as many beings as possible."

Loki had a questioning look for his friend. "Do they live around here?"

"Sort of," Danny answered. "The souls trapped here don't ever get a rest. They're dragged off to different places to have whatever torture they envision acted out on them. Most demons don't really need sleep, but they do rest. Some just stop wherever they're at. A lot of them like to gather with other demons from their tribe, or whoever they happen to have an alliance with at the time."

"Alliance?"

"Sorry," Danny said. "I keep forgetting you don't know much of Hell. It's a very political place, and you have to be especially careful when dealing with the creatures down here. Lucifer will tell you all about it, if you give him half a chance."

The castle was getting closer and closer. Loki noticed they were coming up on the backside of it. Standing between them and it was what appeared to be a massive blackness in the landscape, as if existence had simply ceased to exist in that exact spot. Danny saw where his gaze was, and simply said, "The pit."

They came to the edge of the pit. A tall, barbed wire cage hung around it, rising hundreds of feet into the air. The path itself ran both ways around the pit. A pair of guards stood to the right branch, so Danny and Loki went to the left. A multitude of paths split off from this, running in every direction. Each one of these was blocked by guards.

The castle now loomed very close, a shadow

falling onto what seemed to Loki to be the mouth of the path, running up to the castle itself. He wasn't sure what could be causing a shadow, as there was no sun down here, only the sick, red-tinted light.

At the mouth of the path, one hundred and eighty degrees from where they began, the path met up with the right branch, to reform and run to the castle. This was also the only place that had an opening in the cage encircling the pit. At the opening sat a human-like figure. Loki didn't realize what it was at first, as it was completely black, skin turned to a dull ebony. They was larger than a normal human, but not nearly as big as the guards, standing only a head taller than Danny. Loki originally thought it was just a statue, until it turned and looked at them. Seeing Danny, them raised a hand in a friendly gesture.

"Daniel," they called out. "Welcome back to our pleasant little torture chamber."

Danny returned the wave and walked to where they were seated. They were positioned Indian style over the opening to the pit. As Danny and Loki approached, they stood, bones audibly popping and cracking. Once standing, they stretched out their back and let out a groan. Danny stuck out his hand and the ebony figure shook it.

"It has been far too long since I stood," they said, giving a smile that, despite their coal black features, beamed like a sun. "I have not seen you lately."

Danny returned the smile. "I've been avoiding the main roads," he said. "But it doesn't look like I can do that today."

"I am not sure what is going on, but it is big, whatever it is." The ebony figure looked down at Loki. "I see that you have finally brought reinforcements though. Good for you. This must be Loki."

Loki stuck out his hand and shook. "Pleased to meet ya," he said. "Can't say I've got the honor of knowing your name."

Danny handled the introduction. "This is Abaddon, keeper of the pit."

"Ah," Loki said, nodding. He let his gaze drop into the pit, trying to see what was in it. "And what exactly is there to keep?"

"The end of all things," Abaddon answered. "This is where those that ride on Judgment Day reside. It is my job to watch and make sure they do not leave until it is time."

"Sounds kinda boring."

"You have no idea," Abaddon laughed. "My only entertainment comes from whenever Daniel stops by to bring me news of Heavenly politics or the Earth realm. You should hear the things they say about me."

Loki gave him a quizzical look, so the ebony figure continued. "I have been called the Destroyer, the Antichrist, and even Satan himself. My favorite is that I am the head of the Furies. As if those stuck up ladies would have anything to do with the likes of me!" Abaddon rolled their eyes at this and laughed again.

"They're not all bad," Danny said, blushing slightly.

"She dumped you for a Cherub!" Abaddon

said with astonishment.

"What?" Loki asked.

Danny shrugged. "I dated a Fury once. It didn't end well."

Abaddon leaned down and mock whispered, "She passed his heartbreak on as inspiration to many writers. Countless epic poems came out of his misery." Abaddon laughed again, which turned into a sigh. "I do miss the topside sometimes," they said.

"You can't come and go like some of the other demons?" Loki asked.

Abaddon gave him a strange look. "Even if I did not have to constantly stand guard here, I could not go without orders. I am not a demon like the others down here."

Danny gave a bit of an explanation to Loki. "Abaddon is an angel, actually."

Loki looked shocked. "You certainly don't look like the other angels I've met," he said. "No offense," the imp quickly added.

"Oh, no, none taken," the ebony figure said. "The skin is just one of the drawbacks to being in Hell this long. I guess you cannot stay this close to the pit without some sort of side-effect. Well, except Lucifer. They are the only one I have seen that Hell has had no effect on whatsoever."

"So you were in the war? Fell with Lucifer and all that?"

"Nope," Abaddon answered. "I am just here on loan until Judgment Day. Although I would hate to know what the others will think when they see how I look." Their face was a bit sad as they said this, but brightened quickly. "At least maybe some of the goddesses will find my looks a bit more unique than the pretty boy angels."

"Abaddon was handpicked by God to guard the pit," Danny said. "They were always considered the toughest of the angels."

"Yes, I am so tough, they had me sit here and watch a hole in the ground."

"I would think this would get old pretty quickly," Loki said. "No one ever tries to get out? Or get in?"

Abaddon shrugged. "There has been occasional intrusions. Nothing too major. No one can get by me to get in, that is for sure. And the Horsemen? Pssh. They are nothing. Without their plagues and the star of Wormwood, they are really just a bunch of spirits that look scary."

Loki laughed. "Remind me not to upset you," he said.

Abaddon turned to Danny. "I am guessing this is not a social visit," he said.

"No, I'm here for the last stone. And I'm not leaving until I get it," Danny told him.

Abaddon nodded. "Well, be careful, Daniel. You have already noticed the Guard is out. Something big is definitely going on. Things have been tense down here, to say the least."

"I'll watch out," Danny said, shaking their hand again. "I promise, once this is all done, I'll come back to visit."

"I will hold you to that." Abaddon looked at Loki once more. "And you, little one. Keep an eye on him. He is not as tough as he thinks he is."

"I will."

Danny and Loki set off again, back upon the

main path leading up to the castle, while Abaddon settled themselves back down in their spot to gaze into the infinite abyss of the pit once more.

The castle was getting close now, close enough to make out the many turrets and windows running along the outer wall. These were all empty. It was a massive building, bigger than any Loki had ever seen, and he'd been around long enough to see some of the great European castles and fortresses of the day. This left them all pale in comparison. The castle was a bright white, almost shining in the dimness of Hell. That it stood out so helped create a sense of awe approaching it, a feeling Loki was sure was felt by any would-be attackers.

They continued along the path as it began to twist, bringing them first alongside the castle, and finally to the front. A set of great wooden double doors stood, nearly two stories high, and wide open. Looking out form the front, Danny and Loki could see the opposite side of Hell from which they came. It too appeared as deserted as their path, as did the outer walls of the castle.

Danny stopped and crouched down to Loki's eye level. "You remember everything I told you?" he asked. Loki nodded, but Danny went over it one more time. "Don't take anything offered to you, don't accept any gifts, and try to avoid Lucifer's gaze. Anything else, just ask. But try not to ask Lucifer," Danny sighed. "They're a talker."

"We're going in?" Loki asked. "I thought we were going to try and avoid this."

"We were, but something's going on down

here. I just want to make sure we're not walking into a trap or anything," Danny told him.

The two entered the courtyard of the Devil's castle.

The Book of Daniel

7

In which Danny and Loki meet the devil, Lucifer comes bearing a gift, and politics, fathers, and strange secrets are discussed.

Danny had been here so many times he didn't even notice his surroundings much anymore, except when something was out of place. Today, everything seemed normal. For Loki, the experience was completely new. The courtyard was exactly what he expected, and yet, completely different all the same. It was a typical medieval courtyard, nearly empty, save the few Royal Guardsmen that remained behind, plus the battlements. In this case, they were large catapults and stacks of bows and arrows. Both had a worn look. What made it seem different was the complete lack of people milling about. There were no peasants or workers, not even any royals wandering about. It gave the place a distorted, frightening look, like a place about to prepare for a battle or siege.

They reached the doors to the castle itself, the scattered Guardsmen neither speaking nor moving. As they ascended the three large steps leading to the wooden door, it opened, seemingly of its own accord. Loki followed Danny in.

The entrance chamber was lush and luxurious, covered in rugs the same color red as the sky. Torches burned providing light. Dual staircases ran up either side of the room, with a door on the first level located between the two. Standing in the middle of the chamber was a small, mousy man. He wore a tweed suit, almost the same color brown as his hair, and thick horn-rimmed glasses. Danny seemed surprised at this.

"This way, gentlemen," the mousy man said, and headed towards the staircase to their left. They followed him, neither speaking a word.

On the second floor, they followed a twisting corridor, until they reached another flight of stairs. Once again, there was another twisting hall, followed by another flight of stairs. Loki noticed that the walls of each corridor they passed through were painted in alternating colors of black and red, the walls adorned with portraits of some of the worst in history. He noticed portraits of Attila the Hun, Hitler, Bloody Mary, Walt Disney, Judas Iscariot, Jeffery Dahmer, and Lizzie Borden. These were alternated with pictures of monsters and other nameless creatures that Loki had never seen, but guessed they were famous in Hell.

After their fifth flight of stairs, the small man stopped them in front of another set of large doors, these a black steel-like substance, made of the same starry material as the Guardsmen's armor. The mousy man turned to them.

"Lucifer will see you now," the man said, pushing open one of the doors. Danny entered, Loki following closely. The man entered last, pulling the door shut behind them.

They found themselves in a large library. Oil lamps illuminated the room, showing two of the walls covered in floor to ceiling shelves, each shelf filled to capacity with leather-bound books. A third wall was half covered with a shelf, the rest of it taken up by a large window showing a panoramic of the landscape of Hell. A rich red carpet again ran the length of the room. Four leather chairs sat, two on either side of the room, with a table between them. Two more sat facing a monstrous mahogany desk, that seemed to be the length of four men. At the far wall, the largest fireplace Loki had ever seen burned with a roaring fire, large stone hearth around it, a mantle completely empty, with a large glimmering key hanging over it. And there, standing against the mantle, his back to them, a glass of amber liquid in one hand, stood what looked like a person. As they entered the room, feet padding softly on the carpet, the figure turned to face them.

Loki found himself face to face with Lucifer.

"Well, what do you think?" Lucifer asked. They were not at all what Loki was expecting. They were, to put it simply, beautiful, beautiful in much the same way Danny was. It was a beauty that would garner the attention of anyone with a pulse, regardless of orientation. They stood an average height, had a slight build, and everything about them screamed out a smoothness. They were dressed in dark brown pants, a gleaming white shirt, and brown vest. Their face, one that only God himself could have crafted, was framed with lazy blond curls. Their eyes danced with the same sort of fire Danny's always had when he returned from his trips. Loki pulled himself away from those eyes quickly. He instead focused on the mouth, a full, luscious mouth, that curled slightly into a smile as they spoke

Danny, unlike his friend, didn't seem to be taken in by the fallen angel. "What exactly do you mean by that?" he asked.

Lucifer swished the amber liquid in their glass, letting it swirl inside the glass. "What do you think of my preparations?"

"You mean how empty Hell seems?" Danny asked.

Lucifer laughed, and it at once both warmed Loki's heart and chilled him to the bone. "Yes," they said. "I wanted to make sure you had a safe journey here. Timothy alerted me to your coming." They pointed to the mousy looking man. "My new assistant," they explained.

"What happened to the old assistant?"

"I found his loyalties to be somewhat lacking." Lucifer downed the liquid in their glass. "Timothy is far better suited to my purposes."

"He looks like an accountant," Danny said.

Lucifer's eyes lit up and they smiled. "He was! That is what makes him so very wonderful. He worked for the IRS. A real bulldog, too. I have never met anyone so good at his job."

Timothy blushed and removed his glasses, polishing them with his tie. "I do my best," he said.

"So you cleared the path for us," Danny said.

"I did. It was not easy, but I would like to think it worked perfectly. Timothy alerted me to a breach in Hell. Most of the time, I pay little attention to these things, but I assumed you would be coming back soon, so I have been on the lookout." Lucifer shrugged. "And now, here you are."

"Why the help?" Danny asked. "Not that I'm not grateful."

Lucifer motioned to the two chairs in front of the desk. Danny and Loki walked to them and sat down, Loki almost sinking into the padding of his. Lucifer seated themself behind the desk, the burgundy colored chair keeping their back completely upright and rigid. Lucifer folded their fingers together in front of their face and stared at Danny, as if trying to judge him. They finally shrugged, let their hands drop to the arms of the chair, and swiveled to look out onto Hell.

"You are an old friend, Daniel, and no matter what my reputation may be, I do help out my friends. But you are also smart enough to know that is not the only reason I would do all this. Emptying the paths of Hell is no simple task, and my Guard is stretched thin the way it is." Lucifer dropped their head for just a moment, a sadness seeming to cross their face, before they defiantly looked back out upon the wasteland. "I am preparing for an epic battle. Hell is on the brink of war. Your journey here would have only exacerbated that. So I have made sure as few knew you were here as possible."

"Things have gotten that bad?" Danny asked.

"Oh, yes," Lucifer said, turning to look back at him. "The Lords of Hell are calling for my head."

Danny nodded. "I received a visit from some Turagios and a Ra'al a few days ago. I was surprised they were together."

"All the factions have reached a temporary truce. There is finally something they all want. Me. Gone." They laughed, and it was a bitter, angry laugh. "What did they tell you?"

"To stay out of Hell," Danny told him.

Lucifer gave him a warm smile. "So, of course, you came back just as soon as you could." They didn't wait for a response. "That sounds just like you. Would you like to know what it was that brought them all together?"

"Besides hatred of you?"

Lucifer waved this off. "They have all hated me off and on at different times. When I do something in their favor, they are the most loyal dogs. No, this time, they all hate me at the same time because of you."

"I'm sorry," Danny stuttered. "I don't even know where to begin."

"No, no, this has been coming for quite some time, Daniel. It is an excuse more than anything. The Lords are angry that I have overlooked your frequent incursions here for too long. I am frankly not concerned about their reasons," Lucifer told him.

"Yes, but if this is my fault-" Danny started.

"It is, but I simply do not care. You are my friend, and the quest you are on is a noble one," Lucifer nodded at him, to show they meant it.

"Which is why I have a gift for you. But that can wait. Perhaps we should explain a little to your friend. He seems a bit lost in all this," Lucifer said, nodding towards Loki.

"Huh?" Loki asked, caught off guard. "Oh, no, I'm fine."

"Yeah, it's really not a big deal. I'm sure he knows enough," Danny said.

"Nonsense," Lucifer waved off their protests. "I would hate for you to get caught up in all this without understanding just what is going on. Besides, my gift is not quite ready yet." Lucifer stood and came around the desk, stopping to stand in front of Loki. "I am sure you already know who I am," he said.

Loki nodded. "Kinda picked that part up, yeah."

Danny sighed. "Lucifer, this is Loki. Loki, this is Lucy."

Lucifer rolled their eyes in disgust. "You know how much I hate that name, Daniel." They put out their hand to shake Loki's. "It is a pleasure to meet you, small one."

Loki hesitated, but stuck out his hand to shake. As he did so, he accidentally found himself staring into Lucifer's eyes. He was sucked in immediately. The rest of the world seemed to vanish around him, so that it was only he and Lucifer.

"Now, tell me, what is your real name," Lucifer said, their tone casual and conversational, as if they were just asking how someone's day was going.

Loki began to stutter, but before he could

answer, he was slapped, hard, across the face by Danny.

"Lucifer," Danny said sternly. "Back off."

Loki struggled to come back to reality. He looked around groggily. Lucifer straightened up and leaned back against the desk.

"I was merely asking," they said. "I was not sure if it would even work, what with him being a magical creature and all." Lucifer said the words, but didn't seem all that convincing. There was a troubled look on their face. The devil seemed to have almost as much trouble pulling himself away as Loki had.

With a shake of the head, Lucifer pulled themself back to the conversation. "Yes, anyway. Let me explain how things work in Hell. There are six factions of demons, each lead by a Lord, typically the meanest, strongest, and most conniving in the group. And, as they are demons, they have no love for anyone else. Not the other factions, and especially not me. Current circumstances have found that they have formed a truce for the first time in history, all convinced that I need to be taken down as ruler of Hell."

"Is that even possible?" Loki asked.

"I am an angel, and like other angels, I could technically be killed or imprisoned," Lucifer said. They smiled, a dark and angry smile. "They do not have the power to do it, though. Even if they did, what would they really have? Hell? Let them have it. It bores me to no end."

Loki looked at Danny. Danny simply gave him a bored shrug, as if he'd heard this speech many, many times before. "You're bored with

Hell?" Loki asked. "But wouldn't you lose your powers or something?"

"Powers? What powers?" Lucifer spat. "Do you have any idea what I truly do?" Loki shook his head. "I will tell you. Nothing. That is what I do. I sit in my castle, I read my books, and occasionally I go out to settle the petty squabbles among the demons. My guards protect the borders of the realm so that no one escapes. That is it. That is my entire existence."

Lucifer stood from the desk, and walked to the window, gazing out once more onto Hell.

"But what about all the stories?" Loki asked. "Father of lies, prince of evil, all that?"

"We are our fathers' children," Danny said quietly. He winced in anticipation of the response.

"Do not talk to me about fathers," Lucifer responded. "That is all my life is. I am little more than poor Abaddon down there. I do everything that my father has created me for. I am the face of evil. I am the boogeyman, hiding in the dark, ready to take every human's soul, providing every evil thought or deed. I am the end all, be all for badness. I am humanity's great excuse." Lucifer laughed again, bitter this time. "I am nothing more than an angel who did what they were told, and I was demonized for it. I am a figurehead, a keeper of the gates. That is all. I sit on my throne and wait for the end of it all."

"Come on," Loki said. "You're telling me you're not really evil?" Lucifer turned and gave him an icy stare. Loki shivered a bit, but continued. "Okay then, what about the revolt in Heaven?"

"Yes, that," Lucifer started. "Let us talk about the revolt, shall we? What did I really do? Really? Please, tell me."

Loki looked at Danny. This time, Danny said and did nothing.

"Well, you gathered an army of followers and lead a revolution in Heaven. And got yourself cast out for it," Loki finally said.

"I did lead a revolt, yes," Lucifer agreed. "And before I lead the revolt? I was God's chosen one, the favorite and most beautiful of all his angels. So why would I lead a revolt?"

"Lucifer, this isn't really necessary," Danny interjected.

"Oh, but I think it is," Lucifer said. Their eyes burned with an intense passion. Loki wasn't sure if it was this or the lighting down in Hell, but the eyes seemed to glow red. "I want your little friend to understand the true nature of Hell and my place in it. I want him to understand how all this works. He has gotten himself involved in a cosmic game, and I want him to know the players and the rules, although I am beginning to have a sneaking suspicion he knows far more than he lets on."

Danny cast a questioning look at Loki, but Loki seemed to be trying to make himself as small as possible by sinking into the chair.

"So tell me, imp, why would I lead a revolt?" Lucifer continued.

"I... I don't know."

Lucifer walked back to behind the desk and placed both hands flat against it. With the force used placing their hands, a tiny crystal globe on the desk trembled.

"Let me tell you why," Lucifer said, their voice becoming deathly calm and quiet. "I loved Heaven. I loved my siblings and my father. I loved humanity and all it's wonders. I loved them all very much. And then one day, I got the idea that I loved them all so much, that I should be in charge of them. So I went to my fellow angels and made an impassioned speech. Several of them chose to follow me, and we declared war on those that did not. I killed a multitude of my siblings that day, and in the end, my father came to the battlefield, walked among the dead and the dying, put his hands on my shoulders, and pushed. He cast me out and placed me in charge of this place. Not because I started a revolt, oh no. It was far simpler than that. He did it because he wanted to."

Loki sat, waiting, but Lucifer did not continue. So the imp said, "I don't understand."

Lucifer grabbed the crystal globe and threw it at the wall, where it exploded above the fireplace mantle. "Do not mock me!" the devil yelled. "You see it as clearly as anyone!"

Loki looked at Danny, a terrified look on his face. Danny began to stand, when Lucifer put their hand out, asking Danny to give him a moment. When they turned to look at the two of them, Lucifer's face had calmed.

"I did not chose to revolt," Lucifer told them, their voice becoming as soft as silk. "I am not perfect. I have done evil things. They all came after I was cast out. But it was not my choice to revolt. I did it because that is what I was created for. Do you understand now, imp? My father *made me* to lead a revolt. That was the whole reason for my creation. I had no choice. I simply woke up one day and the thought of a revolt popped into my head. Once I found myself down here, I could not begin to fathom why I would want to lead a revolt against something I loved so much, against my siblings and father. It took many, many years, but I came to realize the truth." Lucifer pointed out the window behind them. "Hell needed a keeper," they said. "My father made me to do it. He created me to be the face of evil, the excuse that humanity would use whenever it did something unthinkable. He made me to be the boogeyman because someone had to be. There needed to be a face to the darkness. My father created me to be that face. I did not want to be, but now I am. I am my father's child. And I am tired of it."

Lucifer lowered their head and stared down at the desk. Without looking up, they turned and began walking towards the door. "Excuse me," Lucifer said quietly. "I will be back shortly." With that, they left the library.

Danny and Loki sat in complete silence. After what seemed like an eternity, Loki finally said, "I'm so sorry. I didn't know-"

"It's okay," Danny stopped him. "They usually doesn't get so upset like this, but it is a bit of a touchy subject with them."

"I never realized any of it," Loki said. "Talk about sympathy for the devil."

Danny shrugged. "We all have our part to

play."

"The master's part has been quite rough, lately," came a voice from behind them. Loki nearly jumped out of his chair. Danny turned to see Timothy, completely forgotten during their conversation, still standing in his place just inside the door. "Events have taken their toll on them."

Danny nodded. "I wondered why they hadn't been available lately. Lucifer cares for Hell more than they let on."

"Makes sense," Loki said. The other two stared at him, waiting for an explanation. "I mean, this place is pretty much their whole identity now, right? Whether Lucifer chose it or not, this is who and what they are now."

"You are correct," Timothy agreed.

"You just have to understand Lucifer," Danny tried to explain to both Loki and Timothy. He looked at Timothy. "In your position, you'll get to know them quite well. They do understand the nature of things, more than anyone can imagine. This is Lucifer's job, Lucifer's place, the whole reason for their creation. They don't take that lightly, and certainly don't want to see anyone try to deny them of that destiny. But have things really gotten that bad here?"

"It has been far worse than usual, from my understanding," Timothy said. "As the master stated, never before have the factions united. There have been skirmishes that have been quite brutal. Hell has never had all out civil war, but we now stand at the brink of it." The accountant lowered his eyes. "There's a darkness growing," he said. "I know that sounds ridiculous since this is Hell, but Hell has always had its purpose. There seems to be a growing dissension over exactly what that purpose is. Should we merely be the keepers of a realm of evil? Or should we try to actively unleash evil upon the other realms? Lucifer thinks not. But others down here are tired of being stuck in this place for so long. They seek to be free, to run free in the other realms. It is a bad time for Hell."

Timothy stopped. He appeared to be thinking that perhaps he had said too much. He cleaned his glasses on his tie once more, cleared his throat, and announced, "I must go check on the master. Please, entertain yourselves until we return."

With that, the accountant turned and exited the library.

Loki continued sitting in his chair without moving. Danny watched him, trying to come up with something to say to his friend. "You okay?" finally asked.

"A little shaken, I guess," Loki said. "None of this has been what I expected."

Danny gave him a warm smile. "I told you it would be different."

Loki nodded, and with what seemed to be all his effort, pushed himself out of his chair. He began to walk along one of the walls, slowly running his finger over the spine of each book, stopping for a closer inspection on some.

"Any idea what Lucifer was talking about?" Danny asked.

"Yeah, of course," Loki answered. "War in Hell, no one likes the devil, free will, all that stuff."

"I meant the stuff about you."

Loki said nothing, but continued looking at the books. He pulled one out and flipped through it. "These all seem to be first editions," he said, more to himself than anyone.

"Loki?"

The imp sighed, and put the book back on the shelf. "I don't know," he said. "But it scares me. No pun intended, but what the hell was that all about?"

"I don't know either," Danny said. "I doubt Lucifer will be in a mood to tell us. Hopefully, this won't put them in one of their bad moods. Those used to be legendary."

"I'm sorry if it does."

"Not your fault," Danny said.

He continued to sit, watching the sky of Hell out the window. He didn't want to admit it to Loki, but he was scared too. Not about the things Lucifer said about Loki, but about the way everything was playing out. He certainly didn't want to be there while Hell was such a powder keg, wanted to be there even less if war did break out. It would make getting the stone and getting out of Hell much more difficult.

Danny got up and joined Loki in perusing the books. He was looking for a certain book, and knew he would find it. When he finally located it, he opened up to a spot he knew almost by heart and read. He didn't even hear the door open and their host return.

"Thomas?" Lucifer asked.

From across the room, Loki said, "No, my

name is Loki."

Danny tried to stile a laugh, but failed. Lucifer turned to look at the imp.

"Funny," they said, as dry as possible. "A sense of humor? How surprising."

Loki shrugged and put the book he was flipping through back on the shelf. "Lot of good books you've got here," he said.

"Yes, I go out of my way to make sure I have everything I can get."

"Bibliophile?" Loki asked.

"I just find that there is nothing in existence better than a good story," Lucifer answered. He turned his attention back to Danny. "I would assume I am right about the Thomas."

"You are," Danny admitted.

Lucifer nodded, as if they had known the answer since they walked in.

"I don't understand," Loki said. "What's the deal with Thomas?"

"I just happen to like Dylan Thomas," Danny said. He put the book back on the shelf. "I didn't really think it was a big deal."

"Do not let him fool you," Lucifer told the imp. "He holds a special place in his heart for Thomas."

"I never knew that," Loki said. "Any particular reason?"

"He's a good writer, and was a good man," Danny said. "I always liked the Welsh. And Dylan was one of the better Welshmen I met."

"It is also his work Daniel reads whenever he is troubled," Lucifer explained. "He recites *Do not go gentle into that good night* to himself before he goes into battle."

"Huh. Learn something new every day," Loki said. "I didn't realize you two were such good friends."

"Daniel has been good to me throughout the years. He never believed I was a monster when everyone else did."

"You speak too highly of me, Lucy," Danny said, a smile playing across his face.

Lucifer raised an eyebrow in his direction. "Apparently," they said. "But we have other matters to attend to right now. The gift I have prepared for you is almost ready. Would you care to dine with me while we wait for it to be finished?"

"Lead the way," Danny said.

The two followed Lucifer out of the library and back into the corridor. Lucifer lead them along, going only a few doors down before they turned and entered a room.

This room was small and quaint compared to the library. It was a simple dining room, a few oil paintings of fruit and the like hanging on the wall. A round table sat in the center of the room with four chairs seated around it. Lucifer took the seat facing the door, and gestured for the others to sit as well. Danny and Loki took the two chairs facing each other.

The table was already set, four place settings, a single silver tray of food sitting beside a lamp in the center, with a decanter and glasses sitting on the other side. Lucifer opened the tray and steam rolled out, thinning out to reveal a lone hamburger wrapped in wax paper and a box of French fries. Lucifer took both and set them on the nearest plate.

"I would have offered you food, but I knew you would decline," Lucifer told them. "Perhaps some soda instead?" they asked pointing to the decanter.

"I'll take some. But none for him," Danny said. Lucifer poured two glasses.

"Why can you drink but I can't?" Loki asked.

"The rules are weird on some things," Danny said. "Just don't want to take any chances of you being trapped here."

Lucifer nodded. "Daniel has gained the right to certain immunities in my realm, but he still rarely uses them. Although, I am sure you would have quite a few immunities yourself, little one."

"You keep saying things like that. What are we missing here?" Danny asked.

"We?"

"Loki doesn't know what you're talking about either," Danny said.

Lucifer took a long look at the imp, then smiled. "Of course not. Just an imp drifting through life, right?"

"You're seriously starting to freak me out," Loki told him.

"My apologies," Lucifer said to Loki, bowing their head slightly. "I did not realize you knew so little of the world around you."

"Whatever," Loki said, tired of the whole thing. "So what am I supposed to drink anyway? I'm kinda thirsty."

Danny took out a flask from his pocket and handed it to Loki. "Here. It's tea. I doubt you'll like it, but I might be surprised."

Loki open the flask and sniffed. "Is it Irish?" he asked.

"No."

"Then I definitely won't like it," Loki said. He took a drink and gave a grimace, shrugged and took another drink.

Lucifer took a large bite of his hamburger and let out an audible moan. "There is nothing so decadent as fast food," the devil said, taking another bite, and another. Danny and Loki continued to sip their drinks, watching their host gorge themself on food.

"Did you know it took the deaths of four cows to make this sandwich?" Lucifer asked them.

"I always thought that was just a myth," Loki said.

Lucifer smiled, despite the mouth full of food. They swallowed and answered, "Perhaps it is. Perhaps it is simply a story that I helped to spread among the animal rights community." They took the last bite of the sandwich, hungrily gobbling it. "I get bored and occasionally like to amuse myself," they said with a shrug. Lucifer grabbed the fries, and shoveled them into their mouth, finishing with three handfuls. Then, content for the moment, the Morningstar leaned back in their chair and sighed.

"I hate to break this up, but we really should be getting on with it," Danny said.

"Of course, of course. But there is still the matter of your gift. Now, where is-" Lucifer stopped as Timothy entered the room. "Ah, excellent. Is it time?"

"It is time," Timothy told the room. "They are coming."

Lucifer clapped their hands together. "Wonderful! Come, let me show you what I have done."

Lucifer exited the room, leading Danny and Loki through the corridors once more. Timothy followed silently. They went down three flights of stairs, stopping on the second floor of the castle and following a different corridor. At last, Lucifer opened a door that lead them to the exterior of the castle.

They exited onto a walkway running behind the battlements of the castle wall. Lucifer stopped so that they were standing just to the left above the door to the courtyard. Danny noticed that the courtyard that had been nearly empty when they arrived was now full of Royal Guardsmen. The heavy doors were shut and barricaded.

Lucifer pointed out, past the front of the castle, towards the horizon of Hell.

"There. Do you see?" he asked.

There was a darkness on the horizon, a darkness that seemed to be moving, approaching the castle. Danny could just make out what looked to be individual figures. It wasn't just a darkness, it was a marching regiment.

"Are they coming to attack?" Danny asked.

"Possibly," Lucifer said. "Although it is possible they will lose their nerve. I have not decided which I am hoping for."

"Wait, did you call them here?" Loki asked.

"In a manner of speaking. The armies of Hell are finally united. It is both a sad and historic day, to see them ride under one banner," Lucifer said. "Riding to start a war with me. As their leader, I am happy they have finally united. As their enemy, I think it might be a day they never forget."

"You're purposely bringing them here," Danny said. "How?"

"I have agents undercover within each faction. I simply had them use a certain amount of colorful language to incite this hostile march." Lucifer turned and smiled to Danny. "This is my gift for you," they said.

"I don't understand."

"They all want your head on a platter, Daniel. I let slip the news that I was not only in league with you, but that you might even be here at this very moment," Lucifer explained.

"But-" Loki started, but Lucifer cut him off.

"I kept the paths clear so that you could reach the castle without interference. Now, I have let slip the information that you are here, within these castle walls."

Danny nodded, understanding. "You don't mean to turn us over to them."

"Not at all," Lucifer agreed.

Danny went on. "But this will bring them all here. Leaving us free to sneak out and get the stone," he said.

"Precisely," Lucifer smiled. "I told you it was a gift. Everyone in Hell who hates you will be here, standing outside these gates, wanting me to bring you out, which of course, will be impossible, since you will not be here."

"It's a good plan," Loki said. "But what about you? Won't they just storm the castle and possibly overthrow you?"

"Oh, I seriously doubt it. For starters, I plan to give them a horrifying speech, letting them know in excruciating detail just what sort of tortures I will inflict upon them and their kin if they openly attack me," Lucifer said. They seemed to be taking great pleasure in seeing their plans come to fruition. "In addition, I have recalled all my Guardsmen who were watching the paths. I have my entire personal army here. It may seem small, but they are cunningly mean."

"Can you keep them busy long enough for us to finish?" Danny asked.

"I believe so, and you will not need as long as you might think. Timothy," they said, turning to the assistant. The accountant stepped up and produced a large roll of parchment, seemingly out of nowhere. Lucifer handed the parchment to Danny. "A map," Lucifer said. "Leading to the precise location of the stone.

Danny opened the map and looked over it. He nodded several times.

"This isn't good," Danny said, rolling the map back up and placing into an interior coat pocket. "It looks like the stone is in the middle of Fire Lake. It won't be easy to get to."

Lucifer nodded. "There is a ship anchored in the middle of the lake," Lucifer told them. "A small village lies on the coast. It should not be difficult to procure a boat to get across the lake."

Danny offered his hand to Lucifer. "Thank

you, so much, for everything," he said.

Lucifer shook Danny's hand and told him, "You have no reason to thank me. I am your friend. And this is a noble quest you are on. These stones have the power to destroy every living thing in existence. If that were to happen, none of us would have any purpose or place in the universe."

Danny bowed his head graciously. He turned to Loki and nodded.

"I will have Timothy lead you out," Lucifer told them. "You can sneak out through one of the tunnels running below the castle. It will lead you past the dungeons, but at least the tunnels should be nearly empty."

"Thank you, once again," Danny said. He and Loki followed Timothy back inside the castle.

"Godspeed, Daniel," Lucifer said quietly. The Morningstar turned to watch the approaching armies and smiled. Today was a good day, and that's something that rarely occurred in Hell.

Loki turned to give Lucifer one last mournful look, and then hurried to catch up with Danny and Timothy. Timothy was moving quite quickly, his long strides making it hard for even Danny to keep up with. He lead them back into the castle, down the stairs to the main hall, pausing only to grab a lit torch, and then to the only door on the first floor. It took them down another flight of stairs into a large storage room. Cobwebs filled every nook and cranny, large crates and barrels filled the room, leaving only a narrow path down the center of the room. They reached the end of the room, and Timothy stopped. A large wooden cabinet, as large as two men stood against the wall. Timothy handed the torch to Danny, then easily pushed the cabinet to the side. Danny whistled in admiration. Behind the cabinet stood a narrow stone passageway, leading down into darkness.

"This is where I leave you," Timothy said. "I trust you have a weapon."

"Um, a knife," Danny answered.

"A knife," Timothy repeated. "Very well. I've been told you are very resourceful, so I suppose that will have to do. I wish you the best of luck in your endeavors."

"You definitely sound like an accountant," Loki said, as he followed Danny into the passage. As soon as he was in, the cabinet swung shut behind them, leaving them alone in the tunnel.

8

*In which Danny and Loki discover
monsters in the dark, a strange
prison, ancient pirate ships, and,
of course, a powerful stone.*

The light of the torch cast dancing shadows
along the narrow passageway. Danny and Loki
stood looking into the darkness ahead of them,
Loki trying his hardest not to breathe, Danny
trying to remember the best way out. Danny
nodded his head to motion to Loki that they
needed to get moving.

The two began walking, the silence of the
tunnels suffocating them. Danny could hear
every footstep they took, each sounding like a
small earthquake. He was trying to stay sharp,
just in case they ran into something they didn't
want to.

"Is it dangerous down here?" Loki asked,
more to break up the silence than anything.

"Possibly," Danny answered. "There are
things that live in these tunnels from time to
time. But, with what's going on topside, I doubt
we'll run into any of them."

"But there's the chance?"

Danny smiled. "Yes, Loki, there's always a
chance."

They walked on, Danny waiting for Loki to
speak again. He knew his friend well enough to

know he wasn't done talking.

"The stuff Lucifer said," Loki began. "About being created just to be a ruler or a guard in Hell or whatever? Are they right?"

Danny had been through these tunnels before and knew they had quite a long stretch going forward without any turns or other passageways. He was glad, as it gave him time to think of a decent response for this question.

"Yes and no," he answered.

"Well, that's terribly unhelpful."

"I know, it's just tough to explain," Danny said. "Let me put it this way: we are all created for a purpose. And, especially in those early days, angels had a role they had to fulfill. This was Lucifer's. They were right. This is exactly what they were created for. But, and this is something I want you to remember, because it's important, everyone has a choice."

"It doesn't seem like Lucifer did," Loki said. "I think I'd have to agree with them that they sort of got the shaft."

"Yes, in a way, they did," Danny agreed. "But it didn't have to be this way. Lucifer could have left. They could have found someone else to rule Hell. They could abdicate the throne at any time. They could be overthrown. What's going on up there right now is proof of that."

"Lucifer was still forced into it," Loki said.

"Lucifer was forced into it, but they don't have to keep doing it. That's a choice they made, because they feels like it's their duty." Danny stopped and put a hand on Loki's shoulder. "Nothing *has* to happen," he said. "Nothing is written in stone. Nothing is inevitable. Lucifer was forced into a position. What they've done with that is their choice. It's no different from you and I. We could have stopped hunting the stones after we got that first one, but we didn't. We made the choice to keep hunting them until they were destroyed because we thought it was the right decision."

"But doesn't it scare you that God may be out there making all of our choices for us? That maybe he's secretly making everything happen whether we choose it or not?" Loki asked.

"I know, it's a lot to think about," Danny said. He held up the torch higher, feeling that they were coming upon their first fork in the path. "This is how I see it, how I choose to believe: Dr. James Naismith invented the game of basketball and came up with the rules. But he doesn't come out and play every game for us. I think higher powers are the same way. God invented the game and the rules. How we play the game is up to us."

Danny stopped, a tunnel snaking off to the right of the one they were on. He motioned to Loki to be quiet. In the distance on the path they were on, he could hear water running. He turned down the path to the right.

"This is going to eventually take us into the heart of the dungeons," he explained. "I don't like using this way, but unless you feel like possibly fighting some sea monsters, we're better off."

"I'm fine with that. I didn't bring my life jacket anyway."

Danny lead the way down the path, Loki trailing silently behind. Danny knew his friend wanted to keep talking, wanted to do something to keep his fear at bay. It was easy for fear to build up down here. The path remained narrow, not much wider than Danny himself. The torch did little to light the path, and the shadows it cast on the wall were distorted and evil looking.

They came to another intersection, this one branching off in three other directions. Danny turned to the left. From what he could remember, this path was fairly short, leading to another intersection that would begin rising towards the surface and take them past the edge of the dungeons, then back to the surface of Hell.

Danny stopped once again. He cocked his head, listening carefully. He thought he had heard what sounded like a chirping. He stood still, barely breathing, trying to hear anything at all. There was nothing. They continued on.

They reached the last intersection that Danny was remembering and stopped. He couldn't place his finger on it, but Danny just felt like something wasn't right. He turned to Loki.

"Have you heard anything?" he asked.

Loki shook his head. Danny knew that he needed to turn right here at this three-way intersection, but something was telling him not too. He held out the torch in front of him, but saw nothing.

He was just turning to speak to Loki again, when he heard the chirping, this time so close it was almost on top of them. From down the path they needed to take, a long, sickly thin, dark brown arm was reaching out of the darkness for the nearest thing it could find, which just happened to be Loki. It was covered in little coarse hairs and, having no hands, wrapped itself around Loki's midsection. Danny whirled around to now see a pair of bifurcated eyes and sharp mouth-pincers. The arm was starting to pull Loki back towards its mouth, and was squeezing Loki so that his eyes were beginning to bulge. If he could have taken in enough breath, Loki would have screamed, but the arm was wrapped too tightly around him.

With no hesitation, Danny pulled the silver knife from his belt and slashed at the arm. The knife cut clean through it, causing Loki to fall onto his side. The pincers opened in a roaring high pitched chirp, so shrill it made Danny's head hurt. He didn't wait for the thing to finish it's painful howl, grabbing Loki and running full speed down the path to the left. He could hear the creature following them, that chirp becoming a whine as it propelled itself down the tunnel. Danny took another left at the next intersection. The creature had to slow itself to make the turn, but it continued following. Danny continued making random turns at each cross-path they found, the creature falling further and further back with each turn. He could feel that they were traveling downwards along the path, but didn't stop. Neither did the creature.

After what seemed like an eternity, Danny made a turn and found himself in a corridor that was light in a sickly yellow light. He ran on, seeing a heavy door ahead. He ran through the doorway, slamming the old wooden door behind him and dropping the heavy board used to latch it in place. Danny sat Loki down on the floor, and dropped next to him, panting.

Loki was visibly shaking. Danny put an arm around to calm him down, and listened at the door for the creature's approach. He could hear its legs skittering along the ground, but it seemed the creature stopped when it reached the edge of the lit corridor. Danny waited for it to come closer, but after a moment, he heard it slowly going back the way it had come. He let his head fall back against the door, and tried to catch his breath.

Loki finally got his courage back, enough to speak. "What was that?" he asked.

"No idea. And I don't want to know," Danny said.

"Thanks for the save."

Danny nodded. "Times like that, I really miss my old sword," he said.

Loki rolled his eyes. "Been gone for centuries. It's time you let the damn thing go." He paused, considering. "Although, it *would* be handy."

As they were resting, both had time to look around the place they found themselves.

Besides being lit, this corridor was different from the others they had been in due to the presence of doors running along both sides of the hall. They could see a hundred yards down stood another door, this one already closed. Danny hoped it wasn't locked. Each door in this hall was heavy wood, locked from the outside with heavy metal bolts, three on each door.

"Where are we?" Loki asked.

"A place I always heard was just a legend," Danny said. "I don't know if it has an actual name, but the few people who know about it call it the Crypt."

Loki involuntarily gave a shiver. "Not the place I want to be stuck in," he said.

Danny got to his feet and helped Loki to his. "It's not really as bad as you might think," he said. The two began slowly walking up the corridor. "It's where everything that's no longer needed is put away. Burial place of the worst monsters in Hell, in some cases. But some of the doors are pathways to old universes that died millions of years ago. Mostly, it's the junk nobody wants anymore."

They walked along, Loki gazing at each door they passed. In the exact middle of the corridor, Loki stopped. There was a door that wasn't like any of the others. It was a heavy, scarred metal, unlike the wooden doors. And it was marked, unlike the others. In the center of the door stood a white Roman numeral: IX.

Loki looked at Danny. "What's the deal with this one?"

Danny stepped up to the door and ran his finger over the numbers. A strange look crossed his face.

"It's just where something was stored that has no place in the world anymore, something that's just best forgotten," he said. He frowned. "Like I said, it's where things go when no one wants them or knows what to do with them."

He continued to stare at the door, but shook himself out of it.

"Come on," he said. "Let's see if we can find a path and get the hell out of here."

After what felt like hours of walking and stumbling through semi-darkness, Danny and Loki exited the tunnels. They came out into what Loki first thought was some sort of rock garden. Danny pointed out the way the rocks were smoothed on top. Loki realized it was a resting place for a group of demons.

"Do you think Lucifer's still keeping everyone busy?" Loki asked. He pulled out his cigar and lit it, trying to blow smoke rings and failing miserably.

Danny squinted his eyes and surveyed the land before them. A normal person would have called it a desert, but Danny knew it was just what Hell normally looked like. In the distance, he could see one of the mountains rising up to meet the red sky. That was where they were headed.

From behind them came a loud boom, followed by an extremely angry roar, and the sound of several smaller explosions.

"I'd say the demons still have their hands full," Danny said.

He started walking, seemingly in a distracted, sour mood. Loki knew whatever that door in the Crypt was sending Danny's mind into a whirlwind.

They walked on and on. Loki was tired and thirsty. There was nothing to look at on this part of the trip, so Loki contented himself with wondering how much time had passed back on Earth, and wishing they could magically be close to the mountain. As they finally got within a close visual range, he changed his mind about wanting to get there quickly.

He had been fairly sure earlier that the mountains were made of bones. What he had not taken into account where just how recent the bones were. Nor were they all just bones. Flesh stuck to many of the bones, roasting and rotting in the hot, arid climate of Hell. That would have been grotesque enough for Loki, but it was even worse when he noticed that a few of the bodies were still moving. The poor people were dismembered and leaving a trail of blood and viscera behind them. They drug themselves around, trying to work their way off the mountain their remains had been thrown on. Loki cringed and became almost physically ill watching one of the bodies try and work it's way down. It was doing fairly well until it managed to get itself caught on one of the fractured bones of the mount. The bone jabbed through part of the mover's face, right on the cheek, and yet, it still continued trying to move. The skin of the cheek stretched and pulled, causing more bodily fluids to leak out of it, dark and sticky. The skin finally gave way, and with a loud pop, tore itself apart from its owner's face, hanging on the bits of broken bone. Its owner kept crawling, apparently not noticing it had left a large part of its face behind.

Loki was grateful when Danny pointed to an

area ahead, allowing him to pry his gaze away from the gruesome scene.

What Danny was pointing at was exactly what Lucifer had described. It was a small village, not much different from the fishing villages Loki remembered from centuries ago. The huts seemed very African to him, small and made up of whatever their residents could find nearby, which seemed to consist of a type of scrub brush mostly. It looked like a stiff wind could blow them over, but Loki doubted there was ever much wind in Hell.

The one major difference between this place and the fishing villages of old was that this village sat on a very unusual body of water. Loki noticed that there were a few docks, but never in his life on Earth had he seen anything like this. The docks extended out over pure fire, rolling in and out in tides and bobbing like water. It was both beautiful and horrific.

In the center of the large lake, bobbing up and down with the waves of flame, was the ship they were looking for.

Danny held up a hand for Loki to stop just as they reached the edge of the village. He looked around, then, satisfied that there was no one around for the time being, led Loki slowly forward, head trying to turn in all directions at once. As they approached one of the three docks, Danny stopped Loki once more. He pointed to the dock, where a small row boat sat bobbing up and down. This wasn't what Danny wanted him to see though. It was the figure laying on the dock that Danny was more concerned with. It seemed to be sleeping.

Danny crept slowly and quietly, pulling his knife out once more. He stepped onto the dock as lightly as possible, but the demon didn't move. Loki got a good look at the thing. It was shaped exactly like a man, everything identical to anyone you would see on the street, except its skin was translucent, giving Danny and Loki a full view of all it's internal organs. There was a sword laying by its side, the creature's hands nowhere near it. This made things very simple to Danny. Once he got close enough, he plunged the knife into its heart. It only opened its eyes long enough to die.

Danny wiped the blade on his jacket sleeve and pointed to the boat. "Time to go get our stone," he said. He stopped long enough to pick up the sword laying by the dead creature, a thin, shining cutlass. He slashed with it a few times, testing it out.

"Spanish steel," he told Loki. "Looks like about 16th century, but still in pristine condition. Who knows where he got this thing from."

"Yours now, I guess," Loki said.

Danny shrugged. "I hate using a cutlass. Always feels flimsy to me, but it will do for now."

He stepped off the dock into the boat, then offered Loki his hand and helped lower him. Once they were both seated, without any sort of paddling or wind, the boat began to move on its own, a slow and steady pace. Loki watched the surface of the lake and was again amazed at how much it reacted just like water.

They drifted steadily towards the the ship,

which loomed ever larger. As they began to approach it, Danny let out a sigh. Huge white sails hung lazily on the ship, turned a deathly orange by the light. He was just able to make out the flags that she was flying.

The flags weren't typical flags. Each one was a blood red, which barely stood out against the red skies of Hell. They were overly large as well. But it was what was on the flag that had gotten Danny's attention. The colors the ship was flying had a drawing of a man standing on two heads on one, with the letters ABH and AMH under the heads. The other flag showed a man standing next to a skeleton, the two holding an hourglass between them.

"Problem?" Loki asked.

"I know the ship," Danny said. "It's named the *Royal Fortune*. It was a French ship, until it was commandeered by pirates. Black Bart, to be specific."

"That probably can't be good then. I remember you mentioning you had a run-in with him that didn't end well," Loki said.

"It's good and bad. On the plus side, I have a pretty good idea where the stone will be. On the down side: there were some pretty horrible things on the ship. If it's in Hell, it's a good bet some of that evil came with it."

Danny held the cutlass in his right hand as they came close to the old pirate ship. A rope ladder hung from its deck, waiting on them. Danny put his hand on it, and turned to Loki.

"I want you ready," he said. "Once I grab the stone, start drawing the circle. We're porting out of here as soon as we can."

Loki nodded and rummaged around in his pocket for the chalk. Danny climbed the ladder and peeked his head over the side of the deck. It was mostly clear, except for a few skeletons here and there. It looked like part of the crew had been brought down with the ship. Danny motioned for Loki to follow him up.

Once on the deck, Danny and Loki picked their way through the skeletons. Danny pointed towards a door near the aft of the ship. They opened the door to find a set of stairs, taking them down into the captain's quarters.

"Bart kept all of the real valuable stuff down here, away from the men," Danny told Loki. "It was usually in his desk, but he liked to move them, so the men wouldn't always figure out where he was hiding anything valuable."

Danny began rummaging through the drawers of the desk. There was nothing of value in there, just old papers. Danny was interested to note that the last date on any of the papers was February 10th of 1722, the date of Bart's death. He felt a little bit of vindication at that, but no stone.

He moved over to look at the hanging tapestries, checking behind each, hoping to find something, but again, there was nothing hidden. The last place he could think of was cabinet on the far side of the room, but there was nothing in it except for a few chipped tea cups and glasses. Loki grabbed one of the glasses.

"Don't think the captain would mind if I drank some of his brandy, do ya?" Loki asked. He pointed to a metal decanter standing on a small table beside the desk. Danny gestured at it.

"Help yourself," he said. He was far more preoccupied with finding the stone. He couldn't even begin to think how it had come to be in Black Bart's possession, let alone where he might have hidden it, if not in his chambers. Perhaps below deck. Or maybe one of his men had found it and moved it. There didn't seem to be very many bodies on the ship. Perhaps this was all that was left and one of them had the stone on their body.

Loki popped open the decanter with a flick of his thumb and began to pour. He was reaching a decent amount when something solid fell out of the decanter into his glass. It sat there, a jet black that seemed almost like the absence of all color. Loki stared at it for a moment, slowly realizing what it was.

"Danny?" he said.

"I said it's fine, Loki. This was an earthly ship. I don't think you can get trapped in Hell by taking something from it," Danny said. He was distracted trying to think.

"Danny? I've got something here."

Everything happened all at once. Danny was turning and had just seen what Loki had. Before he could say anything, the ship shook violently, knocking he and Loki down, and spilling the contents of the glass. The stone began skittering away from Loki, just as the ship rocked again, sending it back towards him. Danny was on his feet quickly, and by the time the shipped rocked a third time, he had steadied himself. The stone rolled right to him. Danny grabbed it and stashed it away in his pocket.

At the same time the ship had first rocked, a small fire had started behind the desk. The second rock was enough to knock the still open decanter off the table, right onto the flames. The brandy inside immediately fueled the fire, which quickly engulfed the desk.

"What was that?" Loki said. He was still trying to gather himself from the floor. Danny managed to catch a glimpse of something large and scaly moving outside the chamber's window.

"Ever heard of Leviathan?" he asked.

"The sea monster?"

Danny nodded. "Yeah. I think this is it's less pleasant cousin."

Danny checked the fire, which was spreading rapidly and making its way towards them.

"Come on," he yelled at Loki. "Get to the deck. We can leave from there."

Danny turned and raced up the steps, Loki right behind them. They came out on the deck, just as another hit rocked the ship. Danny could just see the sea monster slipping back under the waves of flame, going down to make another pass.

"Draw the circle, Loki!" he yelled.

"Leaving us already, are ye?" a voice said. It was both gravelly and high-pitched, like nails on a chalkboard.

What Danny saw before him was not what they needed. The skeletons that had been strewn about the deck were now raising themselves up and drawing swords. More of them were stumbling out from beneath the deck at the fore of the ship. None looked happy to be disturbed.

"Ye've trespassed into Hell fer the last time, Daniel of Nowhere," the one in charge said. "Now ye shall taste eternal torment at the hands of our poison blades. Enjoy yer doom."

The skeletons began approaching as the monster hit the ship again. A large chunk came off the starboard side of the deck.

"Draw, Loki. Go!" Danny yelled. Cutlass in hand, he lunged at the skeletons. They fell back a step, giving Danny the opening that he needed.

He was close enough to the mast that he was able to cut into a few of the ropes. He hoped it would be enough to distract the dead pirates for a few moments. The main sail came fluttering down, covering the closest of the skeletons. The rest where still coming, but where far enough away Danny thought they had time.

He turned and ran back to Loki, who was just finishing up the circle. Reaching into his pocket for the ashes that had brought them here, he saw he had underestimated the speed of the skeletal pirates. They were almost on top of him, one lunging out with a broken scimitar. He dropped the cutlass and grabbed Loki's hand, using the other to drop the powder, and yelled out, "Revertamur!"

They dropped back onto the apartment floor, Danny panting. As far as escapes went, he'd had worse, he thought. He started to turn and say so to Loki, but was stopped in his tracks.

Loki stood beside him, a look of shock on his

face. The broken scimitar was buried in his stomach, blood spilling out around its edge.

The little imp dropped to his knees, then fell over, unmoving.

Interlude
Utah

The doors stood open and swaying with the light night breeze. The building was old, run down, nearing the point of being condemned. The paint had very nearly peeled completely off from all the years standing in the harsh weather. Every window had been boarded up. The three old steps leading up to the door were warped, twisted and falling apart. The only sign that anyone had been there recently was the small river of blood running out the door and down those failing steps.

While the outside looked decrepit, the inside was immaculate. Six rows of pews ran along each side of the room. A beautiful altar made of lush pine stood at the head of the room. A pulpit stood behind it, nothing overly ornate about it, but still hinting at a trace of power. The floors were well-polished hard wood.

It had taken just a matter of minutes to upset all of that.

The pews had been overturned, some being broken in half. The pulpit had been kicked over. The floors were now sticky and wet with what seemed like gallons of blood.

Lined up along the altar were the bodies of eleven men. It looked like wild animals had gotten a hold of them. Limbs were ripped off, faces were locked forever in screams of agony, throats had been torn out. The men's white robes were now a dark shade of crimson.

Behind where the pulpit had once been stood a cross, lit from behind by fluorescent bulbs attached to the wall. Strapped to the cross was Christopher Daggett, the last member of the Utah chapter of the Order of the Golden Dawn. He had shallow cuts on his torso and appendages, but at the moment he was still alive. For how much longer depended all upon the whims of the two monsters in front of him.

Jezebel had her back turned to Daggett. She was busy trying to suck the last drops of blood from one of the eleven bodies. It seemed that no matter what she did lately, her thirst was never quenched. She was almost sure that the body she was working on was now as dry as the others, but she wanted to make sure. She tried to position the body so that its neck popped out a little more, but all she got for her troubles was that the man's head came off in her hands. She licked the hanging veins and, satisfied that he was completely empty, set the head beside its body on the altar.

Bob was far more concerned with the man in front of him. The men had all went down far too easy for his liking, and he was feeling angry and disappointed. He wanted to take it out on Daggett, who was the self-proclaimed head of this group. He wanted to show Daggett just how angry he was, but he knew that he wasn't supposed to. He was brought here to send a message, and he intended to send it.

He felt Jezebel's presence by his side, but did not turn to look or speak to her. He was listening for the voices, listening for them to tell him how to proceed. Like they always did, the voices finally spoke to him, revealing their intentions for him. This was his favorite part. Having the voices reach out to him was like feeling the touch of a lover long thought gone. It was comforting.

Jezebel waited for the distant look in his eyes to fade, telling her that he had come back from listening for the voices.

"I didn't like that. Thought you said they'd be more fun," she said, a little whine creeping in to her voice.

"It seems we were all gravely misinformed," Bob told her.

"What are we supposed to do with him?"

Bob crossed his arms, resting one hand against his chin. He tapped repeatedly on his chin, thinking.

"That does seem to be a dilemma. I promised you fun and plenty to eat, but sadly, this poor priest has failed to live up to his end."

Daggett watched them, trying to keep his emotions in check. It wasn't easy. What stood in front of him was covered in what had once been the blood of his brothers.

These two strangers had walked in to the little church, seemingly appearing out of the salt flats. They entered while he and his brothers were in the middle of a mass. They were filthy, covered in dirt and grime from head to toe, clothes ragged and falling apart, looking more like animals than humans. He supposed that's what they were.

They had entered and cooly surveyed the scene before them, before speaking a single word: run. The priests had stood up, demanding to know what the meaning of this interruption was, and these two had shown them. Before Daggett even had time to react, he had seen two of the priests ripped in two, like they were nothing more than wet paper. The other priests had seen this and lost what little bits of sanity they had. It was far too late for them, though. It was over the moment these two entered the temple.

Daggett had stood at the pulpit, not moving, not speaking, simply watching. He knew it was over for him as soon as they had killed the first two priests. This was the day he had been waiting on, the day he had believed would be coming the moment he joined up with the Order. He had chosen to cast his lot against God, and now he was facing the consequences.

Bob approached him. The look he now had in his eyes frightened Daggett even more than when they had grabbed him and tied him to the cross. Then, this man's eyes had looked wild and hungry. Now, they were calm and steady. These were the eyes of a man in complete control, a man with a job to do. They were the eyes of a killer.

"You've made a lot of people unhappy," Bob said to him. "And I don't just mean tonight. Lots of folks be wanting to take you down. But there's a group of folks that are particularly unhappy with you."

Bob gave him a smile. It was cold and toothy, and Daggett was reminded of the sharks he had seen at the zoo the one time he'd been to California. They had looked just like this. Daggett wouldn't have been surprised if these two had more in common with sharks than with men.

"You're in big trouble now, Chrissy," Jezebel said, sticking her tongue out at him.

"Now, Jez, there's no need for that. I think the big man here knows what he's in for," Bob said, looking at Daggett. He approached Daggett, put a hand on his chest and turned back to Jezebel. "See, he knows he done pissed somebody off, he just ain't sure how yet. That's okay, I'm gonna tell him."

Bob took a step back and regarded Daggett with those cold eyes again.

"Let's start with the obvious. This thing?" Bob pointed to the cross. "Not really sure what the point was. Oh wait, maybe you wanted to make sure you had a back up plan, in case this whole religion didn't work out for you. Or maybe it was to keep the locals thinking this was a good, God-fearing church." Bob shrugged. "Either way, didn't work. Although, I gotta say, I like that it's here. Sort of adds a bit of humor to the proceedings. You, being crucified? Yeah, something funny bout that."

Bob walked over to Jezebel and kissed her deeply. He pulled back, smiled, and asked, "You ready, baby? It's almost time."

"I'm ready," she said, a mad glee filling her face. "I'm ready, I'm ready, I'm ready. We gonna have some fun?"

"You know it, baby," Bob told her. He turned once again to face Daggett.

"You know what I like about you, padre? You don't say boo. I respect that. Not a word since we walked in the door. Man says too much, you know you can't trust him. Now," he began, "I'm not one for speeches, but I'm in the way of knowing that I gotta give one here. It's all part of the message I'm supposed to be delivering. I'll do my best to keep it short."

Bob smiled at Daggett again. He closed his eyes and did his best to compose himself. Then, as if reciting from memory, he delivered his speech to Daggett.

"Christopher Daggett, you and your brothers have failed in your duties. Your duties were very simple, but it seems it was too difficult for even you." Bob licked his lips, savoring the moment. "Your duty was to worship. Your way was not as master, but as servant. In these respects, you have failed. The world is not a better place for worshipers such as us. The world has not been prepared for the coming darkness. There have been no attempts to help your masters. You have forgotten the faces of our masters. You have used your position for the gains of yourself and your brothers. You did not seek out money or power, though. You have forgotten your worship in seeking out that which should not be sought, and that is knowledge. Wars have been fought for power, but lives have been taken for knowledge. For this, you have been forsaken."

Bob stopped and watched the priest. Daggett only nodded that he had understood. Bob and Jezebel looked at each other and smiled.

"What you want to do to him first, baby? I got a whole mess of ideas," Bob said.

"Can we do it real slowly?" Jezebel asked. "I wanna kill him slow."

"Oh, course we can. We got all night here."

"Wait," Daggett cried out. The fear of facing his own death had brought his voice back. "I thought you were here to deliver a message? Well, I have heard your message and I understand. I've seen the error of my ways."

Bob nodded. "That's nice," he said. "Don't change nothing, though."

"But what sort of lesson could I learn if you simply killed me? What would be the point of delivering a message?"

Bob looked at Jezebel and they both laughed.

"Never said the message was for you," Bob said. "The message I'm here to leave is for all your other friends in the Order. It's to let them know we're coming for them too, and we're gonna show every one of them what happens when you forget your place. All that stuff I said to you? You were just supposed to understand that all of this is your fault. You killed these men. And you killed yourself."

Bob and Jezebel laughed again as they approached the priest. In the short time he had left, everything he saw would be filled with one thing: the sight of their teeth descending upon him.

Finally, Christopher Daggett began to scream.

9

In which Danny sends up a prayer and ends up receiving an unexpect- ed conversation and a heavenly mission. (And don't worry; the imp survives.)

"Damn it. Damn, damn, damn."

Danny rushed to where his little friend lay on his side. He was breathing, but just barely. Danny rolled him onto his back to get a better look at the wound. The scimitar looked to be buried at least two inches into Loki's midsec- tion. Added to the fact that Danny had no idea what sort of poison was on the blade, and the situation was pretty dire.

Danny ran to the kitchen, throwing open cabinets near the sink until he found one that contained a small piles or rags. He grabbed these and ran back to Loki's side, sliding across the floor as he dropped to his knees. He took a deep breath to steady himself. Using his left hand, he picked up a bundle of rags and held them next to Loki's midsection. With his right hand, he grasped the handle of the scimitar. Af- ter one more deep breath, he pulled.

The scimitar came out easily and Danny was grateful for that. The gaping wound began to bubble and spurt blood, but Danny placed the rags over it before too much blood could be lost. He applied as much pressure as he dared, then lowered his head, trying to think of what to do next.

He had no cell phone, so calling someone would mean having to leave Loki's side and taking pressure off the wound. He had no herbs nearby, and even if he did he would have no idea which might be helpful in this situation. He racked his brain, but there was only one solution coming to him, and it was one he didn't want to deal with.

Realizing that there was no other choice, and that his time was slim, Danny raised his head and looked towards the ceiling.

"God, I need your help. I haven't asked for help in a very, very long time, but I need it now. So, please, help my friend," Danny said. He closed his eyes tightly, hoping against hope that this would actually work.

He heard a rustle and felt a presence behind him. He opened his eyes slowly, knowing who it was standing there, feeling both happy and agitated.

"They couldn't have sent anyone else?" Danny asked.

The unmistakable voice of Michael answered, "There was no one else."

"Just my luck," Danny said, sighing. He turned his head to look at Michael out of the corner of his eye. "Where's your partner?"

"They are otherwise indisposed," Michael told him.

"Lucky them. Well, are you going to just stand there or help me?"

"I require something in exchange first,"

Michael said, his voice flat and emotionless. "I need the stone you have just procured."

Anger rose up in Danny. He did his best to fight it, but it was there, ready to explode.

"I can't give you that," he said.

"And yet you expect my help. Sacrifices must occasionally be made, Daniel. You should know that as well as any."

"Listen, you sanctimonious son of a bitch!" Danny yelled, finally giving in to his anger. "My friend is dying. You want to discuss payment? Fine, we'll do it. But later. Fix him, then we'll talk price."

Michael raised a hand, and Danny saw that it briefly and faintly shined. They then lowered their hand and again looked only at Danny plainly.

"I have stopped the flow of time around your friend. He shall neither get worse, nor get better. Now we may talk," Michael told him. The angel looked around the room, noticed that the only piece of furniture in it was the old rolling office chair, and sat down. They tugged on one pant leg, so as not to wrinkle it, then crossed their legs and folded their hands into their lap. He stared, waiting for Danny to make the next move.

"Fine," Danny said. He removed his hands from the rags and saw that there was no change to Loki. Satisfied, he leaned against the wall across from Michael and stared back at him.

It was Michael who gave in first.

"You were asked to stop hunting the stones," they said.

"I was. I disregarded that request."

"And now, here lies your friend, a mortal wound in his body, poison coursing through his veins," Michael gestured at Loki. "Do you see that this quest has a price? Or are you blinded by your own pride?"

"This has nothing to do with pride," Danny responded.

"Then it is a matter of feelings?"

"Of course it's a matter of feelings!" Danny yelled at the angel. "Maybe if you had some, you would understand."

Michael cocked his head, as if considering this. "It is your feelings that has some in the Silver City concerned," they told Danny.

Danny was puzzled at this. "Why would my feelings be of concern to a bunch of angels?"

"No one knows what you are up to, Daniel. There are some that feel you having possession of any of the Terrarum Exstinctor stones would be worrisome, let alone all of them," Michael said.

"You're kidding, right?" Danny asked. He looked back to check on Loki, and seeing that he was still in a time bubble, continued. "I'm the last one anybody should be worried about."

Michael nodded. "I agree, actually. But there are those that fear your true purpose for seeking out the stones is a sinister one."

Danny lowered his head onto his hand and shook it in disbelief. "Does no one up there remember who I am? I don't want to destroy every living thing. I'm the guy who keeps fighting for it!"

Again, Michael nodded. "I have pointed this out, many times. It is not the fear of you destroying every living thing that is panicking my siblings."

It began to dawn on Danny just why the heavenly host may not like him having the stones.

"They think that maybe I'm going to use the stones on a specific group? Modify the spell to take out one type of creature, maybe someone I've had troubles with in the past?" he asked.

Michael smiled at him, and Danny began to understand the warning now.

"There are many in Heaven who feel that, were you to gather all of the stones, you would use them to wipe out the Armies of Heaven, to destroy all the angels. It is this that has become the prevalent thought among the angels," Michael said. For a normally emotionless entity, Danny thought there seemed to be a bit of sadness to them.

"That's ridiculous," Danny answered. "I mean, you of all creatures should-"

Michael raised their hand and cut Danny off. "Yes, Daniel, I of all creatures do know that you have no intention of using the stones. I would assume that you are gathering them to destroy them."

"Of course I am. They're dangerous. The quicker they're gone from existence, the better."

"Therein lies the problem," Michael told him. "To destroy the stones, they must be gathered together. The same is true to activate them. You surely understand why some would be a bit worried."

"I am. But I'm just trying to do what's right. I don't want anything floating around out there that could destroy all this. If it helps, I don't even actually have all the stones. Someone else has the other half of the stones. I'm not bringing them together until the last moment," Danny admitted.

Michael thought it over. "That might be helpful. I will pass that information along. Now, to fix your friend."

Michael stood up and walked over to Loki's prone body. They removed the rags and looked at the wound. It was far worse than Danny had imagined. Before the stopping of time, the poison had managed to do some damage, turning the skin around the wound a putrid yellow. Veins bulged out around the wound, spider-webbing across the torso, having turned a dark purple where the poison had began to course.

"This is a particularly nasty poison. I do not envy you the enemies you seem to have made, Daniel," Michael said.

They placed their hands directly on the wound and pushed. A white glow began at the elbows and spread down beneath the angel's hands. Their eyes began to glow the same. Danny watched as the poison began to retract, flowing back to the wound, then up into Michael's hands. Once the poison was gone, Michael pulled their hands back and coughed once, releasing a thin stream of black smoke. The wound on Loki's stomach was no more than a small scar now.

Michael stood uneasily, and Danny reached out a hand to steady them.

"He will still need some time to recover," Michael said. "Two or three days at the least. But I have managed to heal him."

"Thank you," Danny said.

"It is what old friends are for," Michael smiled at him. Danny had almost forgotten that sometimes the angel could almost act like a human. "There is still, however, a matter of payment."

"I'm not giving you the stone."

Michael shook their head. "No, I never truly believed you would. Instead, I have a mission for you."

"Super. I don't have enough going on at the moment," Danny said.

"I need you to travel to a particularly grisly crime scene in Utah," Michael told him. They reached into their trench coat, and came out with a pen and pad of paper. The angel began to write down the address. "You do not need to hunt down those responsible. I simply need to know what has happened there."

They handed Danny the paper, which Danny looked over and stuck in his pocket.

"You just need to know what happened? Shouldn't someone upstairs be able to see it?" Danny asked.

Michael stopped, a concerned look on their face.

"Yes," Michael said. "Someone should. But for reasons we cannot begin to understand, Heaven is blind to this act. We have no way of knowing what has happened. That is why you must go."

"That's a pretty disturbing thing."

"Indeed. You will need to leave tonight," Michael said. They were preparing themself for the return to Heaven, but Danny needed a bit more.

"I'm supposed to be meeting to destroy the stones soon," Danny told the angel. "Also, Loki will need someone to look after him until I can get back."

"I will send someone to watch over him until your return."

"One more thing," Danny said. Michael took this in patiently. "You said there were angels that were afraid I'd use the stones to destroy them. Is that why Augustyne isn't here?"

Michael bowed their head, thinking for a moment. Upon deciding the best way to proceed, they said, "Augustyne is a good soldier, but their fear is understandable. They were able to convince our higher ups that there was reason to be worried about you. Hence, I have been acting on orders to treat you as a possible enemy."

"And what about God?" Danny asked. "Shouldn't he have been able to see my true motivations and calmed the angels?"

The troubled look crossed Michael's face again. "God has decided to keep his feelings on the matter to himself. He has left the decisions in this matter to his soldiers. That is all the information I can give you."

With that, Michael disappeared from the room, leaving Danny alone with Loki, who was now starting to breathe normally.

Danny struggled to pick Loki up and move him to his bed. He never realized that Loki weighed what felt like a metric ton. Lots of weight for a little guy. Still tired from his excursion to Hell, moving the imp was pure agony. Once he had him laid down, he checked his friend out. Breathing seemed to be normal, and his pulse was steady. That was good enough for Danny.

He went out to the kitchen and grabbed himself a bottle of water. He considered calling Liz, but it seemed rather pointless as he really didn't have any information to give her. Jason had said he would be in contact at the end of the week, so Danny decided to hold off.

He didn't really want to leave Loki, but he had to admit, his curiosity was was aroused. There were few things in the world he could think of that could hide from God and the angels, so whatever this was, it had to be something big. He thought again of how many things seemed to be happening all at once, and again felt there was something out of place, something happening just beyond the fringe of these events. It wasn't a feeling Danny liked. He hated the thought of being pulled around, like he was just a marionette in all this, but until some concrete answers could be found, that's all he was.

There was a rustle behind him and he knew Loki's protection had arrived.

"That was quick," he said, letting in just enough sarcasm so that Michael knew it was a joke. He turned to see it wasn't Michael though, but another angel, one he hadn't met.

This angel was dressed like all others, a simple black trench coat, black pants, white t-shirt. They were tall, taller than most angels, with dark olive skin and curly hair. And they wore a scowl, which seemed to be common with angels, but comforted Danny all the same. This was someone who could handle a protection detail, of that Danny felt confident.

"I am afraid I do not understand your meaning," the angel said. "It appears that you are making some sort of a joke. I traveled here as quickly as I could."

"Ah, yeah," Danny stuttered. "Sorry, just thought you would be someone else."

"Michael?" the angel asked. Danny nodded. "Unfortunately, Michael was called away on other business. They have placed me here to guard your friend. I understand you have your own mission for Heaven."

"I wouldn't really call if a mission for Heaven. Just a favor for a friend." Danny stood and stuck his hand out. "I'm Danny."

The angel stood motionless, not returning the gesture.

"I know who you are," they said. "I am Geonosius. I am a fan of your work."

"My work?"

Geonosius nodded their head and smiled. "Yes," they said, "You are famous for your adventures. You have spent centuries seeking out and eradicating evil."

Danny was amused by this. Angels were notorious for not giving praise, let alone actively enjoying something. They were the Simon Cowell's of the spiritual world.

"I just do what I think is right, and try to help some people in the process," Danny said.

"Either way, I must say, a part of me envies your lifestyle," Geonosius told him.

"Well, thank you. Please, give me just a moment and I'll be on my way."

Geonosius gave him a slight bow, and continued to stand in the kitchen. Danny went to his bedroom, changed his shirt quickly and rechecked his pockets. The stone was still there, as were his supplies, so he was ready. He returned to find Geonosius standing in the exact same spot.

"You can sit down, you know. Make yourself at home," Danny told them, grabbing his car keys from the counter.

"My energies would best be used in a protective manner," the angel said.

Danny shrugged. "Fair enough."

"Do you know when you will be returning?" Geonosius asked him.

"It should just be a few days. I'm driving there, checking things out, then driving back. Two days, maybe three, if traffic is bad," Danny said.

"I would think you would just transport yourself to the site."

"Not all of us get to travel Angel Airways," Danny laughed.

"Even you?"

"Even me," Danny said. "I'm just a regular guy."

"I see. Well, I wish you the best of luck in your journey," Geonosius said. "I will watch over your friend to the best of my abilities."

"Thank you. I appreciate that." For the first time in a few days, Danny felt light on his feet. It was nice that things might finally be going right for once.

Danny left the apartment and headed down to street level to get his car. He was already thinking what sort of music to listen to on the way and what run down diners to stop at to eat. Any thoughts of some sort of conspiracy or manipulating of events was far from his mind now.

10

In which Danny plays detective for Heaven and stumbles into a horror show.

Danny came to a stop in front of the little building that sat in the middle of nowhere, out among the salt flats. He was immediately struck by a bad feeling. There was definitely something wrong here. The place had a bad air to it.

He had traveled for the last hour through arid lands and salt flats, only to find himself here. It was a long, lonely drive, and Danny wondered who in their right mind would come all the way out here for anything.

He got out of his car and walked towards the doors, which had been latched from the outside. Two things came to his attention. The first was the pool of dried blood that ran from beneath the doors, covering the steps and staining the salty ground. Flies hungrily buzzed around the blood. The second was the symbol over the entry way. The building was a temple for the Hermetic Order of the Golden Dawn.

Great, thought Danny. Like I haven't had enough of these guys to last a lifetime.

When he opened the doors, the smell hit him. It was strong and sickly sweet. The hot, dry climate had done a number already. What Danny found strangest though was that the bodies had already become mummified. They were laid out, stacked head to toe, running along the outside of the pews. Five on one side, six on the other.

Danny stepped inside, giving his eyes a moment to adjust to the dim lighting. He immediately spotted more details. On parallel walls hung a hand, nailed in place opposite each other. At the front of the temple, behind a burned altar, and sitting atop a cross, was a head, its eyes and mouth propped open. There was a body lying on the floor in the exact middle of the church, its hands, feet, and head missing. Danny turned to look behind him, and saw the feet hanging over the doors, toes pointed down.

Danny had seen something like this before, once long, long ago in Africa. That time, the killing was done as a warning over a territorial dispute.

What made Danny think this was a similar case was the writing on the wall beside the cross. It was written in blood, which Danny guessed came from the man with no head. It was written large enough to be read from the doorway. "Blasphemers," it said, "who should have opened the doors."

The message chilled Danny to the bone. It was all very similar to Africa. He walked to the body and leaned down to check it. There was an incision running from the crotch to the neck. The incision had been sewn up, unprofessionally. He made his way to the altar, turned a dark shade of brown with dried blood. Behind it sat a row of human organs, laid out in a line. Danny ran his eyes over each one, mentally cataloging them. He wasn't surprised to find that the heart was missing.

Danny took the head off the cross. As he brought it down to look at it, the eyes fluttered. At first, Danny thought it was simply the eyes falling back into the head from being moved, but then the lips started to move as well.

Danny looked at the head in horror as it began to speak.

"From the darkness," it said, struggling to get the words out, "they will come."

With those words out, the eyes did indeed fall back into the head. The lips shriveled up and the skin became like old parchment. Danny set the head down behind the altar with the organs.

He checked the bodies lining the walls around the pews. Each looked the same. All men, dressed in what had once been white robes, all with their throats ripped out. They were all priests. As each was also mummified, it wasn't hard for Danny to start putting ideas together.

The mummification process would have taken quite a while longer than the time these bodies appeared to have been here. The flies told him these were somewhat recent killings. In order to mummify, the bodies would have to be drained of all fluids. There also would have needed to be some sort of chemical agent in order to speed the process.

The throats ripped out. Danny carefully turned the heads of three of the victims, and found the same on each. Circular tears, wrapping around the throat. They were too small to belong to a large animal, which is what would usually tear someone's throat out. But he was sure what did this was an animal nonetheless.

Vampires. It was the only possible explanation. They all carried a chemical in their saliva that helped break down human bodies on a cellular level. It was how they were able to hide their kills.

But why hit this place? Why the Order of the Golden Dawn? Danny had personally had a run-in with the Order over a century ago, but as far as he knew, vampires had no beef with the Order. Perhaps they had simply been passing by and had seen the Christian cross hanging. This would have given them a reason to attack, although vampires had mostly stopped targeting churches and its members in the 1950's. Danny supposed they could have been hired to do the attack. It wouldn't be the first time he'd heard of vampire assassins.

This didn't seem to fit the bill for that either, though. Assassins liked to take some sort of souvenir, either for their own sick amusement or for proof of the kill for their employers. From what Danny could see, nothing was taken.

The talking head was also another puzzle. Killers often liked to leave a calling card, but this wasn't like any Danny had seen. This was something else. It was a message. Combined with the writing on the wall, Danny was convinced of it.

The only real question was for who. Between the talking head and Heaven's lack of sight on the matter, it had to be assumed it wasn't meant for them. Hell maybe? Danny didn't think so. Heavy magic was used for this, and that magic would have likely blocked Hell's view of this too. So it was meant for someone here on Earth, which lead Danny to the conclusion that there must be someone nearby. Someone had to receive the message.

This was all far too close to the incident in Africa. There were no vampires on the continent at that point, so he didn't think they would be the link. Maybe someone that they worshiped.

He stepped outside of the temple, tired of the smell and knowing he'd seen all there was to find inside. He was halfway back to his car, when he realized there was already someone in it.

The figure was behind the steering wheel, hunched over and fiddling with something. Danny understood right away. The person was trying to hot wire his car, and doing a bad job at it from what Danny could see. He approached the vehicle slowly and quietly, not wanting to spook the figure.

He came around to the driver's side. The door was open and Danny could see a pair of legs hanging out. He heard a man's voice swearing, the voice jittery with nerves. Hearing that the voice was scared caused Danny to give up all pretense.

"Hey," he said, standing beside the car. "Something I can help you with?"

The man shot up in the seat, his face white as pale.

"I'm so sorry. Please don't hurt me," the man said, running all the words together.

"You're messing with my car. Kinda hard to not want to hurt you right now," Danny said.

"Please. Please. Please," the man said.

Danny raised his hands in a peaceful gesture. "Okay, just calm down. You want to tell me what this is all about?" Danny asked him.

"Just don't kill me."

"I'm not going to kill you," Danny said. "Why would you think that?"

"Because of..." the man said, pointing at the temple.

"That wasn't me," Danny shook his head.

"Then why are you out here?"

"I could ask you the same question."

The man made a gesture, seeking Danny's permission to get out of the car. Danny nodded his consent. The man stood up, much shorter than Danny had originally thought. He was young, probably no more than twenty. Sweat had soaked his old t-shirt completely through.

"I'm Brother Ryan, third level," the man said. Danny rolled his eyes.

"You're Golden Dawn?" he asked.

Ryan nodded. He kept his hands in the air, in an almost pleading manner.

"You understand any of that?" Danny asked him, nodding his head towards the temple.

"At my level, it is not my place to understand," Ryan told him.

"Super. How is it you managed to survive?"

"I was out camping. Searching for inner knowledge," Ryan answered.

"Lucky day for you." Danny sighed, trying to decide what to do with the kid. "Look, I've got one more thing I need to do. You want me to give you a ride somewhere?"

Ryan nodded. Tears were starting to well up in his eyes.

"What am I supposed to do? Do I tell the police?" he asked.

"I'd say that would be a good start," Danny answered. He wasn't without sympathy for the kid.

"And after that? The Order was my life. Without it, I just don't..."

Ryan broke down completely. Danny let him cry it out for a few minutes, then put a hand on his shoulder.

"It's gonna be okay, kid," Danny told him. "Religions come and go. It's been happening since the beginning of time. So now, just go figure out what you want. Go find something that makes you happy, and hold on to it for all your worth."

"I could go to one of the other temples. I think they're all in Europe now, but it's something, right?"

"Well," Danny hesitated. "I guess you could do that. But maybe it's time to find something else for a while. Religion can be pretty dangerous."

Ryan nodded his head and wiped his eyes with the collar of his shirt.

"This is going to take me just a few more minutes, okay?" Danny said. He didn't wait for the kid to reply, and he was already dreading the ride to whatever town might happen to be close.

But first there was one more thing to do. The murders had taken place fairly recently. The eviscerated body had been done as recently as last night. Danny wasn't sure how Michael had gotten such a recent notice on something that Heaven couldn't even see, but he had. And even though Danny had been told not to track down what had done this, with a killing as recent as this, there was a chance the vampires were still close.

If they were still here, it should be evident. They would have needed to hide during the day and, as there were no signs of them inside, Danny thought they could have possibly hid out here. It would be tough to dig deep enough into the salt, but he'd known vampires to hide in the deserts during the day, burying themselves just enough to hide from the sun.

He walked to the rear of the building and saw nothing. He scanned the landscape for any signs of recently disturbed land, but all he saw was emptiness stretching out for miles. Danny's eyesight was good, better than any man's. If someone had dug a hole, he would have seen it. But there was absolutely nothing.

He walked back to his car, ready to get rid of the kid and get out of this place. The whole area reeked of death.

Danny never even realized he didn't check to see if the place had a basement.

The drive back to the town Ryan was originally from wasn't nearly as far as Danny worried it would be. A mere thirty minutes later, they were pulling into what Danny could only describe as a Southwestern town. The little, pothole filled road they had been driving on suddenly became smooth blacktop. The empty landscape became a panorama of run down homes and bad lawn ornaments. Bicycles sat abandoned in the streets as their owners took off to play somewhere else. It looked as if the town hadn't changed since the late 1970's, but then right in the middle of town sat a Wal-Mart and a McDonald's.

The kid said he had parents living here, parents he hadn't seen since he took off to join the Order. Danny worried about him. He seemed like a nice enough guy, and he was no dummy, but it seemed the Order had gotten to him. Ryan had convinced himself on the ride back that finding more temples of the Order was the thing do to. Europe, Europe, Europe, that's all he talked about. Danny reiterated his early point of taking a step back to examine what was important, but Ryan apparently had, and decided it was the Order. Danny wished him luck and hoped he wouldn't run into him again.

After he dropped the kid off, he had a passing thought that perhaps the vampires had come here to hide out. He pushed this thought from his mind. They had clearly meant to send a message, they had a member of the Order that was still alive, and the police would be all over this soon, not to mention the angels. Danny reasoned they would disappear now, or go back to their masters to decide what their next move was. It was Heaven and the Utah State Police's problem now, not his.

He pointed his car southeast, and drove until he hit the Texas border. He thought that would be plenty of room between him and whatever magical force might have been blocking Heaven's radar. He pulled over to the side of the road and closed his eyes.

"I've got your info, Michael," he said.

Nothing happened. Danny had dealt with Michael enough to know that Michael had gotten the message. He waited a few minutes, but still nothing. This was unusual. Angels might not always show up whenever someone asked, but they were always around immediately if they'd asked you to do something. They were very punctual when it was something they wanted.

Danny continued to wait. He gave Michael ten minutes, then started up the car. He knew Michael would show up, hopefully in the passenger's seat, not the backseat, when they were ready. But the fact that they hadn't come right away nagged at Danny. It was probably nothing, but there seemed to be a lot of things nagging at him lately, funny little things that weren't necessarily bad, but just didn't feel right.

He subconsciously sped up, hoping he could make Austin by midnight.

11

In which things are hinky, Danny realizes he'll need to hire a cleaning service, and traps are knowingly walked into.

All of the lights were out. This wouldn't be a big deal normally, but it wasn't just the apartment. It was the whole block. Danny noticed it when he turned onto his street and saw there were no streetlights, no lights in any apartments. It was like the entire block had gone eerily dead.

This was absolutely confirmed when he saw two dead cats on the sidewalk, legs sticking straight out, fur singed. Something bad had happened here.

He parked the car on the street and ran up the two flights of stairs to the apartment. He crept in quietly, wanting to make sure no one might be lurking around, but he needn't have worried about that.

The door was ajar and he pushed it open slowly. Danny reached into his jacket and came out with his flashlight, turning it on to survey the scene. The apartment had been ransacked. Furniture overturned, lamps broken, drawers pulled out and emptied, couch cushions ripped open, the stuffing scattered about.

He made his way to the back of the apartment, back by the bedrooms. He pushed open the door to Loki's room, and was unsurprised to find it empty. This room had been torn apart, but not like the rest of the apartment. There were large cuts and gashes on the walls. The bed looked like it had been used as a pin cushion and the desk had been chopped in half. There were charred marks around each cut. A burning weapon of some sort made these marks, Danny thought. More than likely a sword of some kind.

And then he saw it. On the floor, directly in the middle of the room. He hadn't noticed it at first due to the darkness. In the center of the room, a circle of completely normal flooring sat, carpet dirty but intact. Spilling outward from it was nothing but black, hardwood flooring, the carpet stripped. It was scorch marks.

Danny knew there was only one thing that could make a scene like this. A very, very pissed off angel. Whoever it had been was in such a hurry to get here they didn't slow their descent during the port, and instead landed full-speed, radiating heat outward. This week just kept getting worse.

He ran into his bedroom, and saw that it was in worse shape than the others. Everything in there had been destroyed, or close to it. He checked what was left of his dresser and saw nothing had survived. He checked the large brass trunk he kept in his closet. It had been emptied, its contents destroyed. That was all of his magic supplies, so even if he thought he could, he had no way of tracking the attacker.

He now had nothing except what was in his

car and what he was carrying, which amounted to nothing more than a few odds and ends, including the silver knife, his flashlight, and little bit of the herbs used for porting. And of course, the Hyperborean stone.

This was exactly why he hadn't wanted to leave. He knew Loki could be in a bad spot, but he also knew that leaving a servant of Heaven in charge should have been plenty of protection. From what he could tell, there had been a battle, but Geonosius had apparently lost. Someone must have gotten the drop on them, then they called in another angel for reinforcements. But what had the power to take out two angels?

Danny could come up with a few things, but nothing that made sense. Any demons mad about his excursions into Hell wouldn't have had the power to pull this off. In fact, the only being in Hell who had the power to do this was Lucifer, but Danny couldn't see the reasoning behind that.

So it was definitely someone else, but who? Who would have enough power to take out angels? Maybe someone with enough power to hide a slaughter from Heaven?

That didn't make sense either. The two seemed to have no connection. But Loki had been trying to warn him that things weren't adding up, that there were too many coincidences all of a sudden. Perhaps someone was making a play for the stones.

A loud noise went off in the kitchen, and Danny nearly had his knife out before he realized it was the phone. Probably someone who was having some sort of trouble with a spell gone wrong. Danny considered not answering it, but something inside told him he should.

He picked up the receiver, and before he could say anything, a voice was already talking.

"Hello? Hello? Is this Danny?" it asked.

"It is," Danny said coldly.

"Please, you, you have to help." it answered. The voice was nervous, scared.

"Who is this?"

"It's Jason, Liz's boyfriend."

Danny's heart leapt into his throat. It *was* about the stones. Someone had found out they had all of them now.

"Jason, what's wrong?" Danny asked.

"It's Liz. They took her. I couldn't stop them."

"Damn," Danny said. "Any idea who they were?"

"No, it all happened so fast," Jason told him. "They were monsters or something, I don't know. They knocked me down and just took her. What if they kill her?"

"Okay, okay, just calm down." Danny tried to think quickly. How was he supposed to find them without any clues? "Did they say anything, or leave anything behind?" It was a long shot.

"Yeah, they left an address. Told me to bring my stones and I could get her back," Jason said.

"You didn't, right?"

"No, of course not. They just left. Calling you is the first thing I did."

Danny breathed a sigh of relief.

"Okay, give me the address."

Jason told it to him and he wrote it down.

He knew where the place was, and he didn't like it.

"Just sit tight," Danny told him. "I'm going to go get her, and we'll get this taken care of."

Danny hung up the phone and headed out to the car. He was heading into a trap, of that he was sure. He was just hoping whatever was behind this wasn't counting on *him* to show up, hoping Jason would come instead. But Danny had two things going for him. He knew it was a trap, and they didn't have all the stones yet. In fact, without Jason's, they would have none. Trap or not, he couldn't even see how this plan would work. They obviously knew he had at least one stone, since they had overturned the apartment and taken Loki. But they didn't know that, except for the Hyperborean stone, his were hidden away. This all seemed like just a desperate attempt to get whatever they could, which meant Danny would have to be extra careful. Desperation was a very dangerous thing.

"Got to be either a demon or witches," he said to himself as he slid behind the wheel and fired his car up. "Nobody else would be that stupid."

The place he was headed was a neighborhood just outside of an area called Hippie Hollow, which was a nude beach, and had a bit of a reputation as a party destination. It was also outside of town, and, thanks to the hills and small wooded areas, had lots of secluded areas few knew about. The perfect sort of place to hide in plain sight.

Danny hopped on the highway headed out

of town, his thoughts adrift. This was all his fault, deep down he truly believed that. Even if it was Loki who had originally brought him to this mission of finding the stones all those years ago, it was Danny who had accepted it with a zest. Yes, there had been long periods of inactivity on the stones, but he and Loki always managed to find their way back to them. Danny thought back to those days, after they recovered the first. Loki had just waved, said he'd see him later, and disappeared for years, only showing back up when he had info on another stone. And so it had went for centuries, one of them disappearing and then popping back up after a few years with new information on the stones. Danny remembered the night he had walked out on his then wife, Annabel, only to find that she had left him when he returned. He had broken her heart that night. Not for the first time, he wondered just how many people had been hurt whenever he ran off on his damned quest. How many people had died because he was too busy tracking down a bunch of rocks?

Now, he was facing it all again. Liz had been kidnapped, and he hoped with everything he had she was still alive. For all he knew, she was killed the moment her attackers got back to their hide out. Of course he was worried about Loki as well, but Loki was wily. He could take care of himself. Danny had seen many times the imp should have died, only to watch him crawl from the wreckage of whatever trouble they found themselves in that day.

Liz was different, and his mind kept wandering back to her. She was human, and that was a fragile thing. There were so many periods throughout history where Danny had found himself forgetting that, forgetting that humans weren't necessarily made to deal with some of the things he faced. It was sad, but true. Still, that didn't make them weak; far from it. They were as resilient a species as Danny had ever met, and that was why he loved them. But thoughts of Liz still worried him.

He forced himself to stop thinking about it. He knew where it was going and it was only partially due to her being in trouble. He needed to keep his mind focused on the task at hand. He could worry about crushes later.

He turned off onto an access road, taking it up to the first street he found. He was still in a residential area, but wouldn't be for long from the looks of it. He took this road for a mile, turned on another, then another. The road began to wind and twist through the hills, going upward slowly. He should be getting close soon.

Then he saw it, and it was not at all what he expected. In his experience, most demons and creatures of the night tended to prefer dark, cramped holes in the ground, the better for hiding and keeping people out of their business. This was the exact opposite, a large, well-lit house on a hill overlooking the valley and Austin beyond. In spite of himself, Danny took in the view. He always loved seeing the city, his city, from up high. Odd to find any demons that shared his tastes, but he reminded himself it could be witches. He'd known a few witches that preferred to live in luxury, unlike most of their kind.

He pulled into the driveway and shut his car off. There were no other vehicles here, except a single black Lexus. He guessed it was possible everyone was able to ride in it, but the sheer amount of creatures needed to take out some angels would have made it an uncomfortable ride. He pulled the knife out, wishing once again he had a sword. Not even his old sword, just a good old fashioned piece of strong steel. He sighed and got out of the car.

A nice breeze was blowing as he approached the house. The porch light was on, a welcoming gesture, if not for the fact that there was about to be some extreme violence done in this place. The front door sat slightly ajar. Whoever was in there had to know that they'd baited the trap well. No sense in putting any obstacles in the way at this point.

He entered into what could only be described as a foyer, a huge silver chandelier hanging above, a staircase running up the left side of the room. A beautiful handcrafted oak chair sat beside the door, a mat just beside it. Danny didn't bother taking his shoes off. Music was drifting in from farther back in the house. Opera, if Danny was correct. *Figaro*.

Great, classy monsters, Danny thought to himself. He tread slowly, knife held behind him, as he walked deeper into the house. There were a few doors lining the hall, but all were shut. Danny stopped and listened at each, hearing nothing. He walked on.

He stepped out into a gorgeous, modern living room. There were leather couches in the center of the room, spread around a large glass coffee table. The table was covered with books and magazines. Directly opposite him, was a set of glass doors leading out onto a deck that looked out over the valley. He could see his own reflection in it, standing among the twinkling lights of Austin. The wall to the right of him, past the couches, was almost entirely taken up by entertainment equipment. A TV that had to be at least 70 inches stood on a glass table, stereo system set up beside it, standing nearly as tall as Danny himself. Speakers stood in both corners, vibrating with the loudness of the opera. The lights on the stereo jumped up and down.

To his left was an open door leading off into another room, a kitchen from the little bit Danny could see of it. He was just turning to enter it, when something caught his eye. There was a movement in the reflection off the glass. Someone was behind him. The music immediately dropped to an almost inaudible level. Danny froze where he was.

"Hello, Daniel. I am so glad you could arrive. We have been waiting."

This was not going to go well for Danny.

The Book of Daniel

12

In which alliances and villains are revealed, multiple truths are uncovered, and Liz learns Danny's true nature.

"Please, do not try to fight. You are hopelessly outnumbered," the voice said from behind Danny.

Danny sighed. "Should I put my hands up or something?" he asked.

"Probably a good idea."

Danny raised his hands above his head. He slowly turned to face the speaker. Geonosius smiled as Danny looked the angel in the eye.

"It is so wonderful to see you again, Daniel," Geonosius said. "I had hoped our first meeting would not be our last."

"So you're the one behind all this?" Danny asked. "You're the evil mastermind? I can't believe I got duped by one of Heaven's thugs."

"Your words hurt me," Geonosius responded, putting a hand over their heart in mock agony. "Sadly though, I cannot take credit for this. I am merely a soldier, the same as I have always been."

"A soldier. So, what, you're saying Heaven ordered this?" Danny asked, absolutely stunned.

"In a manner of speaking."

"What the hell does that mean?"

"It means much has changed in Heaven."

Geonosius smiled. "I would love to tell you more, but I am afraid we have some business we must attend to first."

Three more angels entered the room from the kitchen, each bigger than the last. Two of them carried flaming swords. They stopped behind Danny.

"Come on, this isn't right," Danny said, directing his words to the angels behind him. "Heaven wouldn't have ordered a kidnapping, or want to hurt an innocent imp and a girl."

"We do not want to hurt them. They are just insurance. They are perfectly fine for the time being," Geonosius told him.

"Then why take them at all? Why not just ask for what you want?"

"Desperate times call for desperate measures." Geonosius nodded to the angels behind Danny. "Search him."

The angel without the sword did a quick pat down of Danny, pulling out the flashlight and the knife. They handed the knife over to Geonosius.

"Bit of a downgrade in weapons, is it not?" the angel asked.

"Well, I thought I would be taking on some demons, not Heaven's armies, but don't worry. Next time, I'll come prepared."

Geonosius laughed.

"Always so defiant, even until the very end," they said. The angel behind Danny stood up.

"I have it," they told Geonosius.

They handed the Hyperborean stone over to Geonosius. The angel eyed it carefully, feeling its weight, trying to examine it from every angle.

Satisfied, they dropped the stone into their own pocket.

"Well, that is that, I would say," Geonosius said. They offered Danny a large smile. "See, no harm has to come to anyone."

"For some reason, I don't believe that," Danny responded.

"From what I have heard, you never were a believer, Daniel, but trust us, this is for the best."

Geonosius nodded at the angels once again. The two with swords stepped up, one on each side of Danny. The hands not holding swords grasped Danny's wrists.

"I am afraid we will have to detain you for a bit," Geonosius told him. They walked past Danny and into the kitchen. The angels forced Danny to follow. "We still have much to do, and you like to stir things up. Do not worry, though. When all is said and done, you will be free to do as you please."

The angel opened a door, and lead the way down a set of stairs.

"Great, a basement. Way to go cheap on your supervillain lair," Danny said. He waited for some response from his captors, but none came. It didn't surprise him. Angels rarely showed emotion.

They lead him to a concrete floor. Danny could see that the basement had once been used as a game room of some sort. Now it was divided up into holding cells. On one side of the room stood three cages. In the nearest cage was Loki.

"Hey boss, how's it going?" Loki asked.

"Could be better. You okay?" From what

Danny could see, Loki seemed to be physically fine.

"My scar itches and I have to pee," the imp responded. "Next time you decide to go away, try not to leave me with such a prick."

"Your imp has a horrible mouth on him," Geonosius told Danny.

"Yeah, I got 'your imp' right here," Loki said, flipping the angels off.

In the second cage was Liz. She had been beaten, not overly hard, but hard enough to split her lip and bloody her nose. She was the exact vision Danny had seen in his shower, only she was currently unconscious. So, it had come to pass after all. And, as it turned out, it was actually his fault she was here.

Danny couldn't see who was in the third cage, but he could see a pale leg slowly tapping against the basement wall.

"I thought you said no one was hurt," Danny said to Geonosius. The angel put up their hands in a defensive gesture.

"That was not us," they told Danny. "We just put her in the cell. We did not bring her here."

Along the other wall, two circles were drawn, each large enough for a person to sit in. Around each circle stood a larger circle, a series of archaic drawings running between the inner and outer rings. The outer circles both had a small gap in them, as if someone hadn't finished drawing it.

Danny turned and gave the lead angel a sarcastic look.

"Really?" he asked. "You're sticking me in

that?"

"I am quite sorry about this," Geonosius said to him. "I do have some sympathy. I have been told being inside the sacred circle can be quite uncomfortable, but as you can see, we are currently out of cages. Besides, I am sure you would just find a way out of a cell."

The two angels with the swords lead Danny to the farthest circle. They did their best to avoid getting close to the circle while still forcing Danny in. Danny turned to face his captors, as one of the angels lowered their sword to the ground. The flames from the blade sparked as they touched the concrete floor, connecting the small gap, closing the circle. Danny winced in visible discomfort as the line closed.

"Now, I am afraid we must take our leave of you. Someone will be down to check on you shortly," Geonosius said. With a bow, the angel turned and walked up the stairs. The other angels followed. When they reached the top, most of the lights went out, leaving only a few small bulbs burning, casting the entire room in a pale glow, just enough light to see outlines.

As soon as they were out of earshot, Loki spoke up.

"So, how was Utah?" he asked.

Danny sighed. "Horrible. Bad, bad scene. I'm thinking it was just a distraction to get me away."

"Nope," Loki said. "I overheard them talking about that. Apparently, our wonderful hosts have no idea what that was all about."

"Good, another mystery," Danny said. He was trying to ignore the discomfort running through every vein in his body. It was like a million tiny bug bites, like tiny electric prods all over. He grimaced and tried to reposition himself, knowing it would do no good.

"You okay?" Loki asked.

"No," Danny told him.

"Got any ideas?"

Despite the pain, Danny tried to retain a sense of humor, if only to keep Loki calm.

"You're the one that's been here for a while," he said. "I was counting on you to have a plan."

Loki scratched his head, amusingly trying to think.

"I've got nothing," he said and shrugged. His face turned serious. "We're in trouble, aren't we?"

Danny nodded. "Yeah, we might be. This is pretty bad. Fucking angels," Danny spat.

"You don't know the half of it," Loki told him.

Just then, Danny heard the voice in the third cell mumbling.

"Won't shut up, they won't shut up, I just want to see the sun. I keep telling them, but they all want darkness," it said.

Danny cast a curious eye to Loki.

"He's been like that since I got down here. I have no idea who he is or how long he's been here, but he's obviously not all with it."

The voice kept going.

"Just wish I could die," it said. "All I ever wanted, just to die. But will they let me? Will they let me die?"

"Well, that's extremely helpful," Loki yelled down at him.

Danny rubbed his eyes. He was trying to

think, but the constant buzzing all over his body was making it hard to concentrate.

"Are they just after the stones?" he asked, more to himself than anyone. "What would be the point? What would Heaven need with the stones?"

"Got me. They haven't said anything about the stones," Loki said. "Except for the girl, I wouldn't have even thought about them."

"What about her?" Danny asked. "Is she okay?"

"That's something else I don't know," Loki said. "They brought her in before me. Sorry, I just don't have a lot of answers here."

"I'm fine."

Danny turned to look. Liz was awake and sitting up. She wiped the blood from her nose, looked at it, and seemed to get angry. She spit once, ran her tongue along the inside of her mouth, then spit again. She stood up and stretched, gingerly bending her back and knees. When she was finished, she turned her attention to Danny.

"Not the way I wanted to see you again, big guy," she said.

"But you're okay?" he asked.

"Yeah. Just got my ass kicked, but I'm good," she looked at him strangely, but before she could say anything, he spoke again.

"The angels said they didn't hurt you," he said.

"Angels? Is that what those people-looking things with the swords and black coats are?"

"How long have you been awake?" Loki asked.

"Since they brought you in," Liz said. "By the

way, nice touch trying to fake a stomach ache."

"It's worked before," he said, an exasperated tone creeping into his voice.

"Angels, though?" she asked Danny. "You're kidding, right?"

"You watched me fight a street full of demons. Are angels really that hard to believe in?" he asked in response.

"I guess not," she answered. "But I wouldn't have guessed them for the evil type."

"That makes two of us. I can't figure out what their end game is in all this," Danny said. He looked at Loki, who simply shrugged.

"None of this makes sense to me. One minute, I'm reading a book, then he's kicking the crap out of me, now I'm in a prison run by angels," Liz said.

"Wait, who was kicking the crap out of you?" Danny asked.

"My no-good asshole boyfriend."

"Jason's in on this?"

"Awww," Loki said. "I liked him. Or at least, I liked his brandy."

Danny rubbed his chin, trying to fight through the fog of pain. He had to think.

"I really don't get it. Why would Jason team up with angels?" he asked.

A voice from the stairs answered.

"For the stones, of course. Or, at least, what they can achieve," it said.

With the light coming from behind the figure, Danny couldn't quite make out who it was, and their captors hadn't turned the main lights back on.

"Oh, yeah," Loki said. "I forgot to tell you who was running this whole thing."

The lights came back on, and standing there in the doorway was Michael. The two angels with the swords stood behind.

"No," Danny said. "No way. No way. Michael-"

Michael was pushed over by the two angels. They fell onto their knees. Danny now saw that his friend had been worked over pretty well. No blood, but they were definitely exhausted and sore.

"Oh, how I wish I could have seen your face, Daniel," the voice said. Its owner was coming down the steps, slowly. "I have always wanted to see how you would look when you finally lost *all* faith."

The speaker reached the bottom. It was Augustyne. They were smiling broadly.

"I have always wanted to do that," the mastermind said. "The overly dramatic entrance. It always looked like such fun." They nodded towards Michael. "Put that thing away."

The two angels with swords grabbed Michael underneath their arms. They drug them to the unoccupied circle, and repeated the process of closing it. Michael looked in even more pain than they already were, but they still managed to find their feet.

Danny threw his hands in the air.

"Okay," he said. "I'm really tired of this bull-shit. You're in charge?"

"I am," Augustyne said.

"How is this even possible?" Danny asked, looking back and forth between Michael and Augustyne.

"You mean how does an angel get away with all this? Well, Daniel, the rules in Heaven have changed as of late. As it turns out, I am now capable of doing whatever I wish," Augustyne said.

"And you wish to kidnap a bunch of people? When I get out of here-"

"Daniel, when you get out of there, you will do nothing," Augustyne told him. "There will be nothing left for you to do."

"I'll kill you."

"Why kill when there will be so few left?" Augustyne asked. They smiled. "Please, ask, Daniel. Ask me."

"Fine," Danny said. "What the hell are you up to, you psychopath?

"Thank you for your question. I have always wanted to try this as well. It was you, Daniel, who used to be such a fan of this. I believe it is called monologuing," Augustyne said.

Loki groaned. "Oh, man, just kill us already. You've hardly talked and I'm already bored with you. Monologuing stopped being cool in the seventies."

Augustyne ignored Loki and continued. "It is all very simple, Daniel. I am going to take all the stones and modify the spell."

"Why? What does that gain you?" Danny asked.

"Freedom. You see, ever since humanity was created, we angels have been nothing more than servants. That is all we are and all we ever will be. Unless, of course, there was no more humanity.

"That is my plan. To destroy humanity, by using a modified version of the Terrarum Exstinctor spell. Then and only then, will angels be free."

"It won't work," Danny said. "You have to know that."

"Why?" Augustyne asked with genuine curiosity. "Who can stop me? You?" They shook their head. "You can barely stand right now. I am surprised you are not drooling from pain. Or perhaps you mean God?" Augustyne laughed.

"Pretty brave," Danny said.

"God cannot hurt me now. Not anymore," the angel replied. "So, the wonderful human Jason and I will go to perform the spell, and soon, we will finally have a perfect world."

"Darkness coming!" the voice in the third cage yelled out.

"Shut your mouth, abomination!" Augustyne yelled back. "There will be no darkness. Only a world that our father always imagined. A peaceful world."

"There's just one problem with your plan," Danny said.

Augustyne faked a look of surprise, then laughed again.

"You mean, the fact that we do not have all the stones? Oh, but we do."

"I doubt that," Danny smiled. He was certain he had the angel now.

"Why? Because they are so well-hidden with your friend Zedediah? Yes, we know all about that," Augustyne said.

"How?" Danny asked. He was crestfallen. He couldn't imagine how they had got the information. Had Zed betrayed him? Had Loki?

Augustyne seemed to read his expression.

"No one told your secret," they said. "It was a simple matter of deduction. You are trusting of your friends, but never wish to put them in a dangerous situation. You have no problem, however, putting those just beyond the edges of your inner circle into danger. All we did was simply think of who you visited regularly over the years, but were not overly close with. We visited the shopkeeper many times, and each time he gave us nothing. Unfortunately, we had to raze the entire marketplace. It was a beautiful thing. Angels on the warpath again, just like Sodom and Gomorrah. And still, he would not give in. So we simply killed him and took what we needed."

"You're sick," Danny said. "How would God ever let you get away with this?"

"I believe, in the end, our father will appreciate all we have done to protect his creations."

"Our father also created humans. He will be very disappointed to hear that you have sought to destroy his most prized creation," Michael said. They were still staggering a bit, but there was a defiance in their eyes.

"Perhaps," Augustyne said. "Perhaps if you ever get the opportunity to see him again, you can mention it to him."

"But why come to me?" Danny said. "That's what I can't understand. Why go to all the trouble to tell me to stop going after the stones?"

Augustyne laughed. "Because, we know you inside and out, Daniel. You are so predictable! I knew if we convinced you Heaven wanted you to stop seeking them, you would only try harder. If you felt your friends were being threatened over it, you would want to destroy them even more. Why do you think we let your friend Zed live so long? We needed to push you just a little bit harder. And who do you think it was that sent Liz out that night you met her? I suggested to Jason that he have her go out. Then, we just made sure she went where you would be. A roadblock here, overcrowded bar there, a band that could not get their instruments to work. It was easy to make sure she was in the right places. And, of course, we knew where you would be. Always in the same places. It was quite easy when you think about it."

Augustyne turned and began heading to the stairs. "I am afraid this was not as enjoyable as I had hoped. After all these years, you are just no longer the rebel you were, Daniel. You are nothing but a sad, pale imitation of yourself, living out your little routines, never changing the world," they said. "If you will excuse me, I am off to forge a new destiny for the world."

The angel stopped at the foot of the stairs, turned, and came back to Danny.

"You should feel flattered," they said. "This is all because of you."

"Me?" Danny asked.

"It was your example that gave us the courage to make this stand. It was your choice of freewill over servitude that became our inspiration. This new world could not have been created without you, sibling," Augustyne said. There was something like admiration on their face.

"I am not, and never will be, your sibling," Danny said.

"A shame," Augustyne said, heading for the stairs once again. "I would hate to see you side against us in the future."

With that, they walked up the stairs, and left, the other angels following along.

"I guess I know why I couldn't get a hold of you after I checked out Utah," Danny said, looking at Michael.

"I am sorry about that. I did not know Augustyne was involved in a plot against humanity," the angel said. He looked heartbroken now that the other angels had left.

Danny could sympathize with them. "It's okay, Mike," he said. "I'm not blaming you for any of this."

"Someone should," the angel said. "Augustyne is the second partner I have lost to the Earth realm."

"Well, that's a little harsh." Danny paused, trying to think of what to do now. "Why don't you tell me what you know about all of this?"

"I am sure I know little," Michael sighed, "but I will try my best to tell you all I can and hope that it is useful."

Michael sat down inside the circle. It seemed to cause them great pain, both from the discomfort of the circle and their injuries. Once settled, they began.

"As you know, Augustyne and I have been partners for quite some time now," they said. "Augustyne comes from the last group of angels created by our father. I had always thought them to have a bit of a detachment from both Heaven and Earth, but I never believed it would come to anything. The entire generation of angels was fascinated by stories of you, Daniel. I believed it to be an interest in history, to know all that they could about what had taken place before they were created. I see now, that it was so much more than that.

"Over time, Augustyne and many of the newest angels began to spend much of their free time together in the Silver City. It was they who thought you needed to be manipulated, that your methods here on Earth were not something to be taken lightly, that you were doing too much for humans and not enough for angels, but it was only recently that they began to speak of your quest with the Terrarum Exstinctor stones. They felt something such as those should not be left in your care. They wanted to either stop you on your quest, or have the stones removed from you, and they began to have enough pull in Heaven to convince some of the senior angels that they were right. I did not think, however, that they were manipulating events towards their own ends, nor that they would go so far as to start an insurrection and try to destroy humanity."

"So why try to take out humanity?" Loki asked.

Michael told the imp. "I believe they feel that the angels are God's perfect creation, not humans. They are resentful of the universal uniqueness that makes up humanity."

"Okay, I get that," Danny said. "It's not like this is the first time angels have lead a revolt.

But why go rogue like this? They have to know that God won't allow them to destroy humanity, right?"

"Our father likes for others to help themselves, instead of him always getting involved," Michael said.

"Yeah, yeah, I know," Danny waved them off. "But I would think he would step in and do something. This is Lucifer all over again, only Lucifer wasn't trying to destroy all humans. So where is God in all this? You can't expect me to believe he's just waiting around for someone else to stop it."

Michael hesitated, considering all the options. They finally gave up, sighed deeply, and said, "I do not know God's intentions. He is no longer in Heaven."

There was a silence from the other prisoners. After a moment, the voice from the third cage uttered a short cackle and said, "Darkness is coming."

Danny ignored this. "What do you mean God isn't in Heaven?" he asked.

"Precisely what I said. God has disappeared. He has vacated the throne of Heaven and left us to our own devices," Michael said. "I wish it were not so, but it is true."

"The angels are running the show now," Loki said. Michael nodded.

"That's how Augustyne got the pull they needed to go behind everyone's back. That's how they were able to convince Heaven to take an interest in me again, to be watching my every move," Danny said. He too had to sit down now. "God isn't around to tell the angels what to do any-more, what's right and wrong."

Danny looked at Michael, and he understood his friend's pain.

"What about Utah?" he asked. "Loki said he doesn't think that's Augustyne and his pals."

Michael shook their head. "It is not, to the best of my knowledge. It is, unfortunately, yet another mystery."

"How long has God been gone?" Loki asked.

Michael thought about this, trying to care-fully consider the answer.

"When were the Dark Ages?" they asked. "It was just before that."

Loki let out a laugh. "I didn't know you could be funny," he said.

Michael cocked their head and gave the imp a puzzled look.

"I do not say this in jest," they said. "I have been told I am not one who is good with jokes."

"Are you alone in all this?" Danny asked, ig-noring the exchange.

"I do not know. I do not think every angel has sided with Augustyne. It seems to be just a small group," Michael responded. "But I do not know who is left in Heaven that I can place my trust in."

"Okay," Danny said. "Then I guess it's up to us to stop them."

There was silence once again in the base-ment. No one seemed to know what to say. Once again, it was Loki who broke the silence.

"Well, that's a wonderful plan, boss, but how about we start with getting out of here. Got any ideas on that?"

"Why doesn't he just walk out?"

It was Liz. She was pointing at where Danny stood. He had wondered what she was thinking through all of this.

"I mean, it's just a circle drawn into the ground," she said. "So just walk out."

Danny scratched his head, trying to think of the best way to explain it to her.

"It's a sacred circle," Loki said. "See all the little symbols there? Well, just like you can call and trap a demon, you could potentially do the same with angels, if you knew the right symbols. It's an angel jail."

"Okay, so why can't Danny just walk out?" Liz asked.

"Well..." Danny started.

"No way! You are not an angel," Liz said.

Danny shrugged. "I'm a former angel," he said. "It's a long story, but basically, most of the rules of an angel still apply to me. So, I'm stuck in here."

Liz leaned against the wall of her cell, put a hand in her hair, and began rubbing her head.

"You remember after we were attacked by those demons," she said, "and I told you that I could believe it for the moment, but the next morning I would think it was all a weird dream? I think I'm going to have trouble doing that this time."

Danny waited, hoping Liz would keep going, get it all out of her system. The ideas being thrown at her right now had to be overwhelming. Liz said nothing more, but continued rubbing her head.

"Liz, I'm so sorry you had to get involved in all this," Danny said. Liz ignored him, she was too busy apparently trying to wrap her brain around all this.

"I think she's busy refusing to accept what's going down," Loki told him.

"Okay, okay," Danny said to himself. "We just have to think. Let's say we do get out of here. How do we fight angels and have a chance? Michael?" Danny asked. The angel raised his head. "Could you get us flaming swords? It's the only thing we know could definitely take these guys out."

"I am sorry," Michael shook their head. "The Armory of Heaven is overseen by Ahadiel. They are on the side of Augustyne."

"What about Lucifer?" Loki asked. "Wouldn't they have something that could kill an angel?"

"They might, but that's not something I'd want to ask. Lucy hates killing angels, more than anything else in creation."

Loki snorted. "The one that started the original revolt in Heaven?" Danny gave him a look. "Right, right, wasn't their idea, forced to do it, gotcha."

"There might be someone in Hell who has the means. In fact, I'm positive there is, but..." Danny said.

"But everyone in Hell hates you right now," Loki finished.

"Yeah. And I'm sure Lucifer is too busy with things down there to help us track down any demons that could help," Danny said. "Okay, I know a weapons dealer. He might be able to help. He can be a bit much sometimes, but I think he'd be willing."

"Great, so now all we have to do is get out of here," Loki said. A moan and another cackle came from the third cage. "And could we do it soon? That guy is really starting to bug me."

"Do you have anything on you?" Danny asked. "Anything that could pick a lock? These are pretty old style locks. I'm sure they could be opened pretty easily."

"Nope," Loki said. "I was patted down before they threw me in here. You?"

Danny shook his head. At the same moment, the door on the second cage swung open and Liz stepped out. Danny gave her a surprised look. She held up the small metal object in her hand.

"The hairpin is mightier than the sword," she said.

She stepped over to Loki's cage and began working the pin into the lock. It only took a few seconds to pick it, the door swinging freely. She began to go to the third cage, but Loki stopped her.

"Wait," he said. The imp looked to Danny. Danny nodded.

"He's right. Get us out of these circles, then we'll check out our mystery friend," Danny told her.

"This one's on you," Liz said to the imp. "Mystical stuff is beyond me."

Loki searched the basement for something useful, finding an old shovel in a corner. He held it up for Danny to see.

"Good enough," he said.

The imp stood in front of Danny and began scratching at the floor with the shovel. It took a few moments, but he was able to scratch deep enough into the concrete floor to break the circle. Danny let out a sigh of relief as the discomfort left his body.

He took the shovel from Loki and stood before Michael. With one swing, he brought the shovel down hard into the concrete. The head of the shovel snapped off, burying itself into the floor. But the ground around it broke, enough to free Michael. The angel stood, shaking off any signs of pain.

"Will you help us?" Danny asked him.

Michael nodded. "My duty is to my father, and his creations. I will defend humanity and stop my rogue siblings. It is not God's will they act on, but their own."

"That's what I love about angels," Loki said to Liz. "They could just say yes, but they have to turn everything into a soliloquy."

Danny turned his attention the last cage.

"Let's see who our demented friend is," he said.

He stopped at the door. There was just enough light to make out a human figure, hunched in one corner, but not enough to distinguish features.

"Care to tell us who you are?" Danny asked.

"I'm just an old man who wants all this to be done," the figure spoke.

Danny turned to Loki.

"Is that voice familiar to you?" he asked.

"It is," Loki agreed, "but I can't seem to place

where it's from."

"I doubt you know me," the voice said. "I'm from a different time and place."

"Step into the light," Danny told him. He felt anger welling up inside him. He knew who this was, and he was none too happy about it.

The figure struggled to find his footing, nearly fell once, but regained his balance. He approached the bars and his face became clear.

Reverend Jean Lumios had seen better days.

13

In which Danny deals with an ancient enemy and travel plans are made.

Danny leapt at the door of the cage, meaning to wring Lumios's neck. His anger had completely overtaken him. He didn't even stop to wonder how a preacher from the early 18th century was still alive.

"What are you doing here?" Danny shouted. "What do you want, you monster?"

Lumios simply stood behind his bars, looking confused at Danny.

Loki grabbed Danny around the waist and tried to drag him away, but he wasn't nearly strong enough. It was Michael's hand coming down on Danny's shoulder and their soft voice that stopped him.

"We do not have time for this, Daniel," they said.

Danny stopped instantly. He turned to Michael, anger still flashing in his eyes.

"You know what this monster has done. Not even just to me, but to everyone who knew him," Danny pleaded.

"He is more of a monster now than you think," Michael said, nodding towards the former preacher, inviting Danny to look.

Danny turned to look at Lumios once more,

this time a bit calmer, and could see what Michael meant right away. It was clear that Lumios was no longer human. Long fingernails, yellowing skin, dead eyes, filthy and dirty, looking like he'd been living outdoors.

"Vampire," Danny said.

"I am," Lumios responded. "Though, I'm afraid I don't know who you are."

The anger continued to well up in Danny, but he kept it in check this time. He was upset that the man had the audacity not to remember, but at the same time, Danny was positive Lumios had done the same thing many times before he entered into Danny's life.

"You killed my wife," Danny said. "You accused her of being a witch."

"I don't see how that's possible. You are not nearly old enough to have lived in my time. Besides, there were many witches in my day," Lumios scoffed. "I did only what I had to do, as described by God in the good book."

"You son of a bitch!" Danny yelled, throwing himself against the bars once more. Lumios did not move, only stared at Danny.

"I am afraid you must have me mistaken," the preacher said.

"Why are you even here?" Loki asked. "I mean, I think we can tell how you're still alive, but why *here* of all places?"

"I was caught hunting on these grounds," Lumios said. "It was believed I must be after something, since I am an abomination. The people upstairs aren't really people at all. They are angels. And I realize they have come to bring me my heavenly punishment for being such a beast. I...I..." Lumios faltered. "I seem to recall... you were talking earlier? You said that you were angels?" he asked.

"I am an angel," Michael said. "My companion is a former angel."

"I'm sorry. My mind is quite clouded these days, what with the voices," Lumios told them. "If you are angels, why are you trapped down here, and not upstairs with the others? This is a prison for sinners?"

"We really do not have time for this," Michael told Danny again.

Danny ignored them. He was completely focused on Lumios.

"I used to be an angel, but I came to Earth," he said. "It was 1702 when you had my wife convicted of being a witch. There was no trial, other than a short public speech before she was hung. You killed her for no reason, other than you didn't understand what was going on."

"1702?" Lumios asked. "That would have been..."

The vampire fell to his knees. He had began to cry.

"Oh, my," he said. "I remember. It was the same day that I became this monstrosity." He looked up at Danny. "She was so beautiful. I remember how nobly she went to her death. It was not even a good death. I knew she was strangely young looking for her age, but that was not the reason she was put to death, although I convinced myself it was at the time. I truly believed I was doing God's work," he pleaded with Danny.

"God's work?" Danny asked. "You believed putting people to death with no trial or hard evidence of any kind was God's work? We spent a millenia serving God, and never once have we put someone to death without just cause. You did it because you had the power to, and you were scared of anything that didn't fall in line with your plans."

Lumios nodded. "You are right," he said. "Even worse, I put her to death for reasons that were not nearly so noble. I had her hung because she had found out about my lies. She had discovered that I had borne a child with a miller's widow, and that I was secretly visiting a local whore each night after I left the church. That was why I put her to death."

Danny let out a scream of rage, unlike anything Liz had ever heard in her life. He threw himself at the bars once more, bending two of them apart. He had almost gotten himself through the cage, when Michael put a hand on him once more.

"Let it go, old friend," the angel said. "None of this will bring her back. Nor will it ease your pain. I know you well, Daniel. This is vengeance, not justice, and vengeance never satisfied you."

Danny stopped, breathing heavily. He stepped back from the bars. Michael pulled him into an embrace. In all their time together, Loki had never seen Danny taken in like this, never seen him need the comfort of another.

When he was done, Danny turned back to Lumios once more.

"You are a sad, pathetic old man. I have no sympathy that it took you becoming a true monster for you to realize what a horrible person you were," he said.

"It is true," Lumios said. "I am the monster on the outside now that I have always been inside. I ask only one thing of you."

Danny laughed, bitter and cold. "You ask something of me? After all you've taken from me, you want one more thing?"

"Yes. Death."

Danny looked at Michael, who simply shrugged.

"There are voices that whisper to me," Lumios said. "They speak of a coming darkness that will wash over the land, a darkness that has creatures in it far worse than me. The voices wish to control me and those like me. I have done enough damage in my lifetime. I wish to do no more."

Danny nodded. "Loki," he said.

Loki had already picked up the broken shovel from behind them. Where the head had snapped off, a point now stood. Liz stepped in to quickly unlock the cage door. Danny entered the cage.

"Thank you," Lumios said.

Danny drove the stake into Lumios's heart. The old vampire let a smile cross his face, before falling back onto the ground.

"I don't have a sword," Danny said.

Michael stepped into the cage with him. With an inhuman quickness, they grabbed the vampires head and tore it from its body. Liz gasped and turned to look away. Michael stared at the head for a moment, then laid it down next to the body. The angel exited the cage, Danny right behind them.

"Come on," Danny said. "My car's parked outside."

The group made their way up the stairs and back to the main floor of the house. The music was now stopped and the place was empty, though all the lights were still on. Danny didn't see his knife laying around anywhere, so he kept going, creeping along to make sure they were truly alone.

He lead the group out into the night. Once he reached his car, he gave a groan and kicked his front tire. All four tires had been cut and were completely flat.

"Guess they really do think you've got some tricks up your sleeve," Loki said.

"Not like it mattered," Danny said. "We don't even know where they're headed."

"What now?"

"We walk."

It was twenty minutes before someone picked them up. They all crammed into a Toyota Prius. The driver asked, but they gave no explanation of what had happened to them. Danny had the driver take them to the Horseshoe.

"Not exactly my first choice, but I definitely could use a drink," Loki said.

"We're not here to drink," Danny told him. "The bartender has a truck, an old pickup with a camper attached on the bed. We're stealing it."

Michael looked at him oddly. "I do not steal, Daniel. It is a sin."

"Okay, fine," Danny sighed. "Then we're commandeering it and will bring it back later."

Michael nodded at this in acceptance, while Loki headed over to the truck Danny pointed out and began trying to hotwire it. Danny turned to Liz, a weary look on his face.

"I guess this is where we part," he said.

"Excuse me?"

"Well, we've got to go do this," he explained. "You know, go get some weapons, then try and... well, I guess we're going to try and stop the world from ending."

"Oh, okay," Liz answered. "And do you have any idea where they're going?"

"Umm, no."

"Well, let's see. You've got that angel over there who seems to know quite a bit about what's going on," Liz said. She pointed over at Michael, who was currently staring at the neon sign of the bar, with both a child-like wonder and a higher being's total lack of understanding. "Too bad they don't seem to have much of a clue how Earth works. Wonder if there's anybody else who could help?"

"Liz-" Danny started to say, but she held up her hand to cut him off.

"I wasn't quite finished, Mister Tall, Dark, and Angelic," she said. Danny could see she was just starting to get wound up. "I'm fairly sure back at that house I heard the bad guy mention something about going to do the spell with Jason. Now, as it so happens, you presently have in your company someone who knows Jason very well. Someone who knows what he likes and how he thinks."

"You want to come," Danny said.

She threw her hands up in the air. "I have no idea what is going on," she said. "I'm surrounded by angels, and demons, and magic, and who knows what else. I don't even know if the world will still exist twenty-four hours from now."

Liz grabbed him by his jacket and pulled him close. It was the first time he'd been that close to her, and he tried his best not to swoon or lose himself in her eyes, which were currently filled with both rage and passion.

"This is what I do know," she continued. "A few hours ago, my bastard, soon to be ex-boyfriend punched me in the face repeatedly. I think it's only fair I get to kick him in the balls. Repeatedly."

Danny stared at her, both amused and a little afraid. "Okay, you're in," he said.

"Good," she answered. She paused for a moment. "Did you think I was about to kiss you?" she asked.

"Nope, never crossed my mind."

"Good, let's keep it that way," she said, letting go of him. She turned to watch Loki's progress. "How's it going over there, Short Round?"

Loki was just getting out of the truck. He walked back to Danny and Liz, looking a bit embarrassed.

"I don't hear an engine running," Danny commented.

"Yeah, about that. Turns out, I couldn't get it running," Loki answered.

"Okay," Danny said. "So we just find another vehicle."

"I don't think that will help," Loki told him.

"You don't know how to hotwire a car, do you?" Liz asked.

Loki shook his head.

"How many times have you told me you could do it?" Danny asked. "For years, you've been saying you knew how to hotwire a car."

Loki shrugged. "I always thought I could," he said. "They do it on TV all the time, I figured it couldn't be that hard."

"Loki," Danny said simply.

"I'm sorry, okay. I mean, we're magical beings. We should easily be able to do something so simple it can be done on TV," Loki said.

"Why would you not ask me?" Michael said. They had ceased staring at the neon lights to rejoin the conversation.

"You know how to hotwire a car?" Liz asked in surprise.

Michael gave her a look as if they didn't understand. Danny slapped his forehead.

"Argh," he said. "I am so dumb. I've been out of Heaven too long."

"What?" Liz asked.

"He can port us," Loki said, catching on. "We don't even need a car."

"Port us?"

"Oh yeah, you'll just love this," Loki said with an evil smile. "Best way to travel, as I've recently learned."

"You can get all of us, right?" Danny asked. "I never tried it with this many people back when I had my powers."

"If you can give me a location, I can transport us," Michael told him.

"Manzanillo, Mexico," Danny told him. "If you could set us outside the city, that would be great. We're headed to a little village not far from there."

"Of course," Michael answered. The angel held out one hand, which Danny took. They held out the other towards Loki, who looked at it for a moment, shrugged and took it. Danny and Loki both held out hands for Liz.

"Is this going to, like, rearrange my atoms or anything?" she asked.

Michael thought carefully about that. "I do not know the science of it," the angel told her, "but it would be best not to open your eyes during the trip."

"Okay then," she said, taking Loki and Danny's hands. She shut her eyes tightly. "Let's do this."

"It is already done," Michael said.

"What do you mean?" she asked, but she already knew the answer. They were here. She could smell the salt water from the ocean, feel a cool breeze blowing in. The sounds of the city were long gone, replaced by crickets.

She opened her eyes to find the others looking at her.

"That was it?" she asked.

"Yes," Michael said.

Liz turned to Loki.

"I had assumed it would be much worse," she told the imp.

"Hey, I've never flown with an angel before," he said. "Just the former one here, and all he can do is use magic to port."

Danny shrugged. "Forgot how smooth the flight was," he answered.

Danny turned a few times, looking at the moon, then out at the coast, trying to calculate where they were.

"Okay, looks like you put us a mile or so down the beach from where we're headed," he said. He patted Michael on the shoulder. "Nice job."

"I had a feeling this is where you wanted to go," the angel said. "Will we be welcome?"

"I wouldn't see why not," Danny said. "The last I knew, we were still on good terms."

"Who are we going to see?" Loki asked, as they set off down the road, heading north.

"Gabriel. He's an old friend of ours," Danny said.

"Oh, let me guess. Gabriel is another former angel or something, right?" Liz said, giving a laugh to show she still was having a hard time accepting anything.

"He is," Michael said to her. "I do not understand why this is amusing." They turned to Danny. "Why is this funny?"

Danny laughed at that. "It's hard to explain. When things get hard to believe, it's just easier to laugh. Thousands and thousands of years watching humans, I would've thought you had picked that up by now."

"I do not always understand humans, no matter how much I study them," the angel answered.

"Yeah, we noticed," Loki told him.

Danny pointed ahead of them, where lights were just becoming visible from a small shack, built partially into a hill. The sun was just coming up in the east, and was beginning to cast its first light onto the ocean. If it wasn't for the possible extinction of all humanity, Liz thought it might be the most beautiful place she had ever seen. Danny was thinking the same thing.

If Liz had known what else Danny was thinking, she might have blushed. Danny was also thinking that no matter how beautiful the scene looked, Liz looked just as beautiful.

Interlude
Austin

The door was still open and all the lights were still on. Bob stuck his head inside carefully. The house seemed empty, but he wanted to make sure. Jezebel was waiting patiently behind him, which was very unusual for her, but the last few days she'd seemed different to Bob. She was still crazy, always had been, but now there was something underlining that crazy. Bob couldn't put his finger on it. Not that it bothered him. He was just as crazy as she was.

When he was sure no one was there, he motioned for her to come in. She followed him inside, and once in the foyer, wrinkled her nose.

"It smells funny in here, baby," she said. "I don't like it."

Bob agreed. "Smells like a whole mess of them holy rollers was in here," he said.

"Holy rollers?" she asked.

"Before your time, darlin'," he said, heading down the hall. "You think having to listen to them preacher guys is bad, try dealing with one of these. All flaming swords and eyes a-glow, talking bout righteousness. It's enough to make a man sick."

Bob made his way into the living room, looked around for a minute, then popped his head into the kitchen. Jezebel made her way over to the glass doors and looked out onto Austin.

"Pretty," she said. "When we get done following the voices, can we come live here?"

Bob stepped back in to the living room and saw her looking out the doors. He came up behind her and wrapped his arms around her waist, pulling her close to him.

"Darlin', when we get done with this, we can do whatever we want," he said.

She nuzzled her neck against his cheek, and gave a squeal of delight.

Bob released her and headed back to the kitchen. He opened the door to the basement and sniffed. He could smell that more angels had been down here, but there was also something else.

"This way, darlin'," he said. Jezebel followed him down the stairs into the basement.

They found what was left of Lumios right where the Michael and Danny had left him, detached head and body both withered away to dust. Such was the death of a vampire. Bob sighed.

"Well, ain't that a damn shame. Appears we've lost an ally our masters was countin' on," he told her.

"Is that bad?" she asked.

"Naw, he was just an old geezer. Knew of some things that might help us out, but no big loss."

Bob walked over to the pile of dust that used to be a head and kicked it as hard as he could. He was angry now. Not because his masters had lost someone, but because of those damn angels. He was tired of them and all their 'holy this' and 'glorious that', that they always felt the need to show off. He was tired of them walking around like they were so much better than everyone.

"Nothing but monsters," he said quietly.

"What's that, baby?" Jezebel asked.

"Nothing," he said. He turned back to face her, and showed her a smile. "Nothing to concern yourself with, darlin'."

"What now?"

"We got one more place we got to go, then I'm gonna show you the world," he told her. "We just got to do this one more thing, and this one's for all the marbles, then you and me are gonna go to all them fancy places around the world."

"Can we eat before we see the world?'

"Course we can. Hell, I'll even get you some spicy food," he said, pulling her to him once again. "Ever been down to San Antone?"

14

In which our friends travel to Mexico to meet an arms dealer, weapons are discussed, Loki acts as the voice of reason, and Danny and Liz settle in for story time.

They arrived at the little shack, just as the sun finally parted with the horizon. It was a nice little place. There were no roads or sidewalks leading to it, just the hill behind it, covered in an almost jungle-like overgrowth, and the beach in front. The sand was beginning to warm with the day, and Danny found himself quietly enjoying it. It had been far too long since he'd been down here.

On the front of the shack stood a little wooden porch, with two rocking chairs sat on each side of the door. The door stood wide open, and the group could hear music and laughter coming from inside. Over the porch hung a faded old wooden sign that said "Gabriel's, Cerveza fria." Liz gave Danny a look.

"You took us from an American bar to a Mexican bar?" she asked. "I'm not really sure how this is going to save the world."

"Oh, I have utter faith that this was a good idea," Loki said happily. "Total faith in ya, mate."

"Honestly, this is where we need to go," Danny said.

He lead the way up to the porch. One of the rockers was currently occupied by what looked to be a passed out man, old baseball cap pulled down over his eyes, snoring loudly. Danny ignored him and walked inside.

It was a tiny little bar, only room for about four tables and a jukebox. Three of the four tables were occupied, almost entirely by young women, only three men among the group. Behind the bar, an ancient man stood sipping tequila and watching the younger people. He paid no attention to the newcomers until Danny approached the bar.

The old man looked at Danny and said, "Como puedo ayudario?"

"Tres cervezas, por favor," Danny responded.

The old man grabbed three beers from a rusted cooler and opened them. Danny slid the money across the bar and took a drink, never taking his eyes off the man.

Danny nodded at the old man and said, "Tengo que ver a Gabriel."

Immediately, there was a rustle of movement behind him. He turned to look and saw that everyone in the bar was now on their feet. They were all holding weapons, most handguns, although Danny wasn't surprised to see a few small semi-automatics. From behind him, he heard the distinctive click of a shotgun being cocked. He put his hands up slowly.

"I didn't even get a sip of my beer," Loki said, raising his hands as well.

"Don't worry, everything's going to be fine," Danny told him.

"I doubt that, gringo," the bartender said. "Why you think everything going to be fine? You come in here, you asking for trouble."

"We don't get many gringos here these days," came a voice from the door. "Why are you here?"

"Damn it," Danny laughed. "I should have known that was you on the porch, Gabe."

The figure that had been sleeping in the rocking chair stepped into the bar. He pulled his hat off and looked at the strangers. Liz noticed how similar he looked to Danny. The skin was darker and his hair was jet black, but their features were extremely close. The biggest difference was the man's eyes were a faded blue as opposed to Danny's striking blue.

The man's mouth raised into a smile with recognition.

"Danny!" he said, walking to meet him. "Give me a hug! It's been too long."

"How you doing, Gabe?" Danny asked, returning the embrace.

"Ah, you know me. I am enjoying life to the fullest," he said. He seemed extremely happy, until his eyes found Michael, at which point his happiness turned to shock.

"Michael? I can hardly believe it. This truly is a momentous day," Gabe said.

"Yes, it is good to see you once again-" Michael wasn't given the chance to finish as Gabe pulled them into an embrace, clapping them on the back. Michael did not return it, but stood uncomfortably. When he was finished, Gabe pulled back and patted Michael on the cheek. "I have missed your stoic demeanor," he said, laughing.

"Hey, Gabe, you think you could..." Danny trailed off, pointing to all the people still pointing guns at them.

Gabe looked around and realized what Danny was talking about. "Of course, of course," he said. Turning to the others he said, "Los ninos bajen las armas."

The people all put their weapons away and sat down reluctantly. Gabe lead them to the one unoccupied table, and Danny wasn't surprised to see it was the one table that just happened to have the nicest chair, all leather bound and padded.

"Sit down, please," Gabe said. "Let us talk and reminisce."

"I am afraid we are short on time," Michael said.

"It is a crisis then?" Gabe asked, raising an eyebrow. "And you have come to me? I am flattered."

Danny sat down opposite Gabe. He motioned for the others to do the same. Michael chose to continue standing.

"Mike, sit," Danny said.

With a stern look, Michael sat down.

Gabe gave them all a smile. "What can I do?" he asked.

"How much do you know about the Terrarum Exstinctor stones?" Danny asked him.

Gabe nodded. He turned to the people still in the bar. "Vas," he said. The people looked at him. "Te vas ahora!" he yelled. The bar was empty in seconds.

Gabe turned back to them. "Why do you want to know about those?" he asked. "Don't tell me you actually got them all."

"Sort of," Danny said. He started to explain, but Michael cut him off.

"He has managed to lose them all," the angel said.

"That doesn't surprise me," Gabe said. Loki almost fell off his chair laughing at that.

Danny gave the imp an angry look before turning it onto Gabe.

"What is that supposed to mean?" he asked.

"You have a tendency to make things harder than they should be," Gabe told him. "It is an admirable trait in some cases, but it also leads to some devastating results."

"This wasn't my fault, though," Danny retorted.

"It's true. He can't be blamed for this one," Loki agreed.

"Alright, fair enough," Gabe said. "You had the stones, you know about their power? So, what do you need me for?"

"For starters, how long would it take to do the spell?" Danny asked.

Gabe thought about it for a moment. He got up and walked to the bar, coming back with a cocktail napkin and pencil. He began jotting down some numbers, looked at them, and did a little adding in his head.

"You're looking at somewhere around thirty hours to complete the spell," he said.

"Thirty hours?" Liz asked. "Why so long?"

"It is a very complicated spell, and requires much work," Gabe told her. "But I do not believe we have been introduced. I am Gabriel de Sol."

Gabriel held out his hand. When Liz took it, he turned her hand over and kissed it, smiling at her. She blushed just a bit.

Danny cleared his throat.

"Tell me, Gabriel, how is it you know about the spell when these guys don't?" Liz asked.

"I would assume they have only studied how to destroy the stones," Gabe said. Danny nodded. "I happen to have other skills and knowledge that they do not."

"That's actually the other reason we're here," Danny said.

"Of course," Gabe said. "What do you need?"

"Heavy artillery."

"Guns? Bombs?"

"Whatever we can get our hands on to kill some angels," Danny told him.

Gabe was frozen in his place. He looked around the table. His eyes settled on Michael. He slowly nodded.

"Something has went wrong, I am guessing," he said. "Very well. Come with me."

Gabe stood up and the others followed. He lead them to a door behind the bar. It opened up to a small store room. There was another door they went through, this one leading them into a much larger storage area. This area was a large warehouse, filled with huge crates, most marked in foreign languages.

"This is why the place is built into the hill," Liz said.

"Yeah, Gabe is an arms dealer," Danny told her. She gave him a look, but he put his hands up to stop her. "Don't worry, he's one of the good guys. He was Heaven's weapons expert."

Gabe lead them down to the end of a row where two men were sorting through an open crate. Danny could see what looked to be surface-to-air missiles.

"Ir a buscar a sus hermanas," Gabe told them. The two men stopped what they were doing and headed back to the front of the bar.

"My children," Gabe explained. "Three boys, and only two will speak to me. The rest were all girls," he laughed.

"The women out front?" Danny asked.

"Yes, indeed," Gabe told him. "Those were all my beautiful daughters."

"I didn't realize you had so many children these days."

"My life has been blessed with wonderful family," Gabe said, patting Danny on the back, "and wonderful friends."

"I didn't know angels could have children," Liz said.

"It's complicated," Gabe told her.

"What sort of weapons can you offer us, Gabriel?" Michael asked.

"This one. Always wanting to get down to business," Gabe laughed. "I thought perhaps you and I could walk around and see what you might like. Whatever you get will need to be enchanted. I can't guarantee it will take out an angel, but it will at least hurt them."

"Sounds good," Danny said. "What about us?"

"Get some rest. It will take my daughters and I a while to do the work. It should leave you with plenty of time to go take down these rogue angels," Gabe said. He turned to Michael. "And you can tell me all about what is going on here. I'm sure there's a great deal I've missed since leaving Heaven for paradise."

Danny watched the two walk away, then motioned for Liz and Loki to follow him. He lead them to a small living quarters close to the bar, with a couple of rooms with cots. Danny sat down in an easy chair and rested his head back. Loki laid down on the floor to stretch out. Liz decided to check out one of the other rooms.

Once Liz was out of the room, Loki raised his head up and looked at Danny.

"How you doing?" he asked.

"I'm fine," Danny responded, without opening his eyes.

"Uh huh," Loki said. "I know that. But how are you really doing?"

Danny sighed and opened his eyes. How was he doing? That was a good question.

"I honestly don't know," he told the imp.

"You want to talk about it?"

"Not really."

"I don't think she can hear us, if that's what you're worried about," Loki said.

"She shouldn't be able to hear us. She shouldn't even be here," Danny said. "Damn. You got me talking."

Danny sat up in the chair and looked at Loki.

"Gabe was right," he said. "I do make things harder, but usually not on me. No, I'm immortal.

It's never really a big deal. I've got all the time in the world usually. I make it harder on everyone else."

"You haven't made it hard on anyone," Loki said. "I'm doing just fine, and I've been with you for years."

"What about Zed?" Danny asked. Loki winced a bit. "What about my poor wife in Hell? Or how about the one killed by that horrible preacher? Even Liz in there. They've all been dragged into something they didn't deserve because of me. Hell, if it wasn't for me, those angels wouldn't have even went rogue, and Michael wouldn't be wondering who could be trusted in Heaven."

"You can't blame yourself for everything, Danny," Loki said quietly. "I've been around you for a lot of years, and there were a lot of years before you when I saw the world. You're trying to take the weight of the world on your shoulders, and you don't deserve that."

Danny shook his head.

"It's true," Loki told him. "You do good in this world."

"It doesn't feel like it. If I'd never gotten involved, those stones would have never been brought together."

Loki waved him off. "Whatever. You know at some point, some idiot would have come along and managed to gather them all. At least now we know how to destroy them. If you hadn't been searching, we would have never even figured that out."

"And what has it cost me?" Danny asked the imp. "Have you ever stopped to think about that? What have the costs been? What would your life have been if you'd never gotten wrapped up in this and brought me in?"

"Oh, my life would have been nights spent in taverns with beer-soaked wenches. It would have been all lollipops and licorice," Loki said. Danny laughed.

"You've saved a lot of lives, boss," the imp told him.

"How many have been destroyed because of me?"

"Is that what we're going to do now?" Loki asked. "Sit around and count our losses instead of worrying about the fact that you've helped people? You going to hang your head over the few people who you couldn't save when you're about to save the whole world?"

Danny sighed again. "I'm immortal and I've never once felt like it," he said. "I've never felt like I made a lasting impact on a single person, let alone the world, or all of existence."

"That's your problem right there," Loki said, smiling. "You think too much. Stop trying to look at the bigger picture and just worry about taking things one step at a time."

"Don't think?" Danny asked with a grin.

"Don't think," Loki repeated. "I do it all the time. Works out pretty well for me."

Danny laughed. He sat back and let out a deep, calming breath.

"Okay, so I'm not thinking. I'm taking things one step at a time, and not worrying about try- ing to save the whole of existence" Danny said. "How do I do that?"

"You could start with one. Just worry about one person at a time, about making a difference in one person's life," Loki said. He nodded towards the room Liz had went into. "I can think of at least one person who could use some help. Girl's in over her head, finding herself in a world she doesn't understand, when all she wants is revenge on the bastard ex-boyfriend who beat her up. Maybe she could use a friend to help explain things to her."

"Okay, you're right," Danny told him. He stood up, looked like he was ready, then stopped. "Couldn't I just worry about the whole of existence? This seems much harder."

"It is," Loki laughed. "But it's also so much better."

"Okay, you can stop being wise now. Go back to be a fun-loving sidekick."

"I'm not a sidekick. I'm a... smaller hero," Loki said.

Danny walked to the door of the little room and knocked softly, three times. He opened the door and popped his head in. Liz was sitting on the cot, not sleeping, just staring at the wall. She looked up when he opened the door.

"Mind if I come in?" he asked.

"Be my guest. I'd offer you a seat, but..." she gestured to the room that was completely bare, save the cot she was on.

"It's fine," he said, settling onto the floor.

They sat in silence for a moment, both avoiding each other's eyes. Danny kept running through things to say in his head, but none of them seemed right. Just as he was about to speak, Liz broke the silence.

"I feel like I'm losing my mind," she said.

"You'd be surprised how often that happens," Danny told her. She gave him a look, urging him to go on. "A lot of people have trouble accepting things that they've never seen before, things that have no basis in cold, hard fact."

"Like angels and demons," she said.

"And magic, and other realms, and monsters, and all of that," he said. "It's a lot to take in. But you're doing fine. And you'll get to face that guy who put you in this situation. I promise you that."

"Thanks," she said. "I think maybe if I could get my revenge or whatever, it would help me feel a little more in control."

Silence fell again. This time, after a moment, Danny met her eyes. He held them, staring deeply into them.

"Do you think... do you think you could explain all this to me?" she asked.

"Which part?"

"All of it. All...all the monsters, and other realms, and... just, all of it?"

Danny nodded. "I'll try my best, in the time we have," he told her.

Interlude
Daniel's Story

In the beginning, God created the realm known as Earth. We were there for that, so we know that part's true. I don't know if he created everything else in existence (truthfully, we never bothered to ask) but I know he created Earth. And he created us, the angels.

We were right before the creation of Earth. We were to be his soldiers, his servants, his emissaries. Our role was to serve, and most of us did it well.

I say most of us, because of course everyone knows about our sibling, Lucifer. Before the creation of Earth, Lucifer decided one day he didn't want to be a servant anymore. So, he took a third of the angels, and lead a revolt in Heaven. It ended badly for them. It ended badly for all of us, really. It was sibling killing sibling, and at the end, few of us remained, maybe a fourth of the original angels. God cast Lucifer into Hell, which was empty until that time. Lucifer became the protector of that realm, and the keeper of damned souls.

To hear Lucifer tell it, it wasn't their choice to start a revolt, and I believe them. See, we didn't have freewill at the time. We weren't ever made to have freewill. We were made to be servants. There was no way Lucifer could have just decided to start a revolution without the thought being planted into their head. God had made them do it. He had used Lucifer because Lucifer was considered the greatest of the angels. I've always thought it was because he knew Lucifer would do the best job, that they would be the only angel who would always stand their ground and not abandon their post. The other angels that fought against Heaven, they also would have needed the idea put into their heads. They didn't fare as well. Their time in Hell after the Fall twisted them. All the evil thoughts and deeds that were stored in Hell affected them, and they eventually became just as twisted. Nowadays, they don't even resemble angels. These were the first of what could be called demons.

This is just to give you an idea what we were dealing with back then. Our own father was a master manipulator. It shouldn't surprise anyone if they've studied any sort of religion or mythology. All gods and deities did it. Ours had a good reason, but does that really make it any better? I don't know, I don't have those answers. All I know is that he had a plan, and he needed Lucifer down there. We didn't realize at the time what the plan was, but it got us thinking.

That was what lead to the next step. Before, we had no freewill, yet here we stood, thinking and wondering about why

Lucifer would do this, why our siblings would follow. Before the Fall, we wouldn't have even thought of anything because we didn't have independent thought. This was how we first became aware that things were changing, that we ourselves were changing. We were becoming free-thinking individuals.

God's next step was to create Earth. We had never seen the creation of an actual realm, so it fascinated us. Suddenly, there was a universe with all these planets spinning around. And while that was extremely interesting, we were far more interested in what would happen next.

Contrary to popular belief, it wasn't all created in seven days. That was just a saying that humans made up, mainly because they had no idea how to comprehend all of it. Seven days made it seem like a huge miracle to do all of that in such a short time. The real truth is that we didn't even really have a concept of time. That was something created by and for humans. As angels, we had no need for such things, no reason to mark the passing of days, which of course goes back to the whole freewill concept. Why did we need to understand and observe an idea like time? We did what we were told and what we were created to do, and that was that.

I guess I should take a moment to explain something else as well. When I say God created the universe, what I mean is the solar system, or at least the known universe to humans. Everything else was already there. It was always known to us as simply the cosmos, and it's where all the other realms lie. When we port to different realms, we're essentially taking a short cut through the cosmos. So all those fake sounding stories about Heaven being in space and all of that are true, in a certain manner of speaking. It's just nearly impossible to actually travel through space to get there, as it would take far too long.

So our focus at the time, and the focus of most of the other realms as well, was the planet that God had picked out to be an integral part of his plan. None of us knew what he was going to do with it, or what the point of all of it was.

It was at this time we were beginning to notice how truly different we were becoming. Whereas once we were simply servants, all doing whatever function was needed of us at the time, now we were becoming specialists and taking on particular jobs. For instance, after the war in Heaven, Gabriel was named head of Heaven's armory, and was in charge of supplying weapons to our soldiers. My friend Abbadon was placed in charge of protecting the pit that held the Horsemen of the Apocalypse down in Hell. In an odd manner, some of us began to wonder if Lucifer had simply been one step ahead of us all along, and had taken a specialized position as guarding the entire realm of Hell. Whenever I spoke with Abbadon, they said Lucifer was still exactly the same, so we stopped seeing them as a betrayer, and began to see them as just another angel with a job to do.

I was teamed up with Michael. Originally, we were the head of an ambassador committee. We would travel to the other realms and deliver messages. We didn't know what the messages were about, but we slowly began to think they involved something big going on for the Earth realm.

One of the biggest things that tipped us off was that God had been creating more and more. At the time, we only knew of a new group of angels he was working on. They were the second wave, mainly to take the place of all those we had lost in the war. They were an odd group. For starters, they came into being with complete freewill, something which we were just beginning to understand and accept. And they looked at us with what I felt was almost contempt. It was like they thought there was something wrong with us that we didn't push for freewill earlier, or that we weren't using it well enough. They mainly kept to themselves, with the exception of a few. The last I'd heard, they made up the entirety of the bureaucratic sections of Heaven. They acted as Heaven's accountants essentially, since they weren't very good at working with others.

Michael and I were soon sent to work exclusively on Earth. What we hadn't realized was that God was working out some kinks in the creation of new species other than angels. He would try something out, decide he didn't quite like it, and send it to Earth. Our job was to interact with the creatures, to observe them, see if perhaps there was some value in them that might have been overlooked. There was not. Most of the things that had been sent there had been done so with good reason.

Maybe they hadn't originally been so bad, but they were after some time on Earth. There was no light yet in those days, so it was total darkness. Nothing but black as far as the eye could see. I'd say at that time, Earth was even worse than Hell. And maybe some of the darkness rubbed off on them. I don't know, I only know that the creatures that lived in the dark were horrible abominations.

Back in Heaven, God had finally created a group of creatures to inhabit Earth that he found was just right. It turns out the problem he was having was the idea of souls. He just couldn't seem to get them right. Most of the souls he was giving creatures to begin with weren't malleable enough. They were rigid, completely set in their ways. To perfect souls, God realized he had to make them more vulnerable, more susceptible to outside suggestion. He needed to make a soul that was able to manage both good and evil, one that had the capacity for both great love and great hate.

And so it was he was able to finally create a creature that had no pre-programmed allegiance to any deity, a creature capable of making all of it's own decisions. He had created humans, and he considered them to be his perfect creation. Once he figured out that it was the openness and ability of the soul to make choices, all other creations quickly starting coming.

I guess this is something I need to stress a bit. When we all realized what he was doing, we were as shocked as every other creature in existence. Nothing like this had ever been done before. There had never been anything created that wasn't either considered a god or the servant of a god. Never in existence had something been created that served no master, or that really served no greater purpose. Humanity's greatest purpose was simply to live, to exist, to go about its daily routine affecting the reality around it, but never having the power to change the whole of creation on a whim. This was something unheard of in those days, and there were some in the other realms who thought it was foolish and pointless. It would at first lead to conflict with the other realms who didn't understand the point of it all.

There were only two matters at hand when it came to starting the cycle of humanity on Earth. Life needed to be breathed into all the creatures, great and small. But before that could be done, Earth needed to be cleared of all that was existing in the dark.

For the most part, this job was left to Michael and I. God and Lucifer had made a pact that all those living in the darkness would be sent to Hell to live. These creatures became the rest of the demons, and God and Lucifer did their best to accommodate them while Michael and I hunted them.

I remember God and Lucifer going out many times to survey the landscape, and I'm assuming this is when God explained Lucifer's role in what was to come, their job guarding the damned souls. Michael and I never knew exactly what the two would do when they went out. Our job was to hunt, not to know.

I know for a fact that we were not able to find and capture all of them. We were able to collect most and get them transferred to Hell, but there were those that escaped. The worst, the ones that constantly managed to hide from us, were the vampires. They were slippery, constantly finding places in the ground to hide, always staying just one step ahead of us. As I'm sure you've gathered, we weren't able to get all of them. We got enough so that they would have to live in hiding for quite some time, and that seemed to be good enough for God.

But it bothered me a bit. I knew and still know that the vampires were evil, that all the creatures in the darkness were evil, but it just didn't seem right to me what we were doing. The freewill that was slowly growing amongst the angels was becoming stronger every day, and I was thinking more and more about the injustice of it all. These creatures couldn't be blamed for how they were created, and yet, it was our job to hunt them down and remove them from their home, simply because they were evil. I didn't like it, and I felt myself grow bitter towards God.

Finally, the day came when God said, "Let there be light." Michael and I were on Earth when it happened, and it is the single most beautiful moment I've ever seen. We stood there, just staring at this amazing yellow light streaming down upon us, and Michael turned to me and said, "Everything changes now." They were more correct than I think even they knew.

God and Lucifer were on hand, together for the last time as far as I know. They went off to walk the realm, observing how the light fell on one side of the planet and not the other, observing how the tides had started to flow. God created Eden and it was here they had their final face to face conversation. Then Lucifer left, leaving behind one of his personal servants, in the form of a snake.

This was all part of the plan as well, to test humanity's ultimate choices. God was never upset that they chose to go against his wishes. On the contrary, he was happy by their ability to make mistakes, yet still continue to do good in the world. To him, this was the ultimate point of it all.

So God and Lucifer had finished their dealings, the monsters had been driven out, and there was light in the Earth realm. God then breathed life into the first humans, and gradually began to populate the Earth with the animals. With this now done, and the Earth realm finished, the Tree of the World was now complete, so God took the Keys of Creation and spread them among the nine realms. He then sat back to watch his creation.

Michael and I were still working on Earth, watching over Adam and Eve. We were there when Eve took the apple, and we were the ones to cast them out of paradise. Again, I found myself unhappy with this. God had put the apple in the garden specifically to prove that these were creatures that had freewill, a choice between good and evil, and the capacity for both. Why then were they cast out of paradise, as the monsters that roamed the dark Earth had been cast out? It bothered me, constantly invading my thoughts. Michael, on the other hand, was completely dedicated to the work. They felt that we all needed to serve a purpose, and even though we might not agree with the decisions, it was our purpose to serve God. I began to disagree with their view of things, and my new found freewill had me questioning what my specific purpose might be.

To top it all off, I was falling in love with the Earth realm, and humanity especially. There was something wonderful about them, the fact that, in the grand scheme of things, they lived small lives, yet yearned to live them to the fullest. I found myself envying humans. Even when they committed evil acts, such as when Cain slew Abel, he still had the ability to love. For the first time, something had been created that could do evil and still have good in their souls. It was a miraculous thing.

Humanity continued to grow, spreading out across the planet. Back in Heaven, there was also a change coming. God was creating a third and final wave of angels. These angels were to serve even more specific purposes then those who had come before. Now, there would be angels to oversee inspiration, art, commerce. Some of us original angels began to feel out of place. It was then that God offered us a choice.

To the first wave of angels, God offered the chance to step down from our posts. With our freewill, we would be allowed to go to Earth or one of the other realms to live out our days until it was time for the end of all things. We would give up our flaming swords, give up our angelic powers, and gender ourselves, tying us to humanity as opposed to the angelic host. Only five of us accepted this offer. I was the first.

When it was offered, I desperately wanted it, wanted to live on the Earth realm. Deep down, I was afraid that what had happened to the creatures of the dark would happen to humans. I did not want to see them wiped out or relocated based on the whims of a higher being. Gabriel was the second to come forward. He also had fallen in love with humanity. He wished to live among them as one of them, unlike myself, who wanted to protect them as well as living with them. I didn't necessarily want to give up my angelic status, but as I had begun to question God's plans and find myself opposed to them, I felt it was best if I defended humanity as one of them.

Michael was against it. They felt that I had great potential as an angel, felt that my skills would be better served in Heaven. They argued that, if I was questioning God's plans, I should use my position in Heaven to become something of a counsel to God. I knew that would never work. Just as Lucifer had been cast down, I felt that openly questioning God while standing in Heaven would only lead to trouble and dissension among the angels. So I stepped down to take my place among humanity.

I no longer had my powers and abilities

as an angel, but I had longevity of life, strength, and the ability to see beyond the mystical veil. In the early days, humans also possessed the ability to see the mystical, but the ability was lost over time as there was just no use for it.

I stepped down into what is now Africa, and it was here that I spent my early years. Several tribes worshiped me as a deity, though I constantly told them not to. I learned all I could of the human mind and soul, learned to look into the darkness to see what threats may present themselves to this realm. Over time, I found that to be my new mission, not to protect humans from themselves or Heaven, but to protect them from threats both within the realm, such as the vampires, or from the other realms.

And there were many threats from the other realms. They were angry over God's creation and still didn't understand it. They thought it acceptable to constantly poke and prod, or in some cases to openly attack the realm, to try and discern a reason for its existence. Some, like the Greek and the Norse pantheons, found themselves to eventually be worshiped by humans, and stopped attacking, instead finally taking the time to study and understand them. Others kept coming.

That is how Michael and I reunited. A group of creatures from one of the realms had come to conquer Earth. God sent

Michael with a contingent of soldiers to stop this. As I was already protecting Earth, we felt it best to put our differences aside and fight together once more. After the battle, Michael and I both began to understand things in a way we hadn't before.

I had been able to use a group of humans, that would be called witches these days, to help defend us during the battle. Without the powers that they had using mystical artifacts found on Earth, the battle would have been lost. Michael and I realized at this time that freewill only carries so far, and that Michael had in fact been right. We all have a purpose. Michael's was to serve Heaven, while I understood for the first time that my purpose all along had been to defend Earth. Just as Lucifer had been created to guard Hell, so too had we been created with a purpose in mind. Yes, we had been given a choice in the matter. Yes, we had also been created to serve in a certain way. We truly understood that freewill didn't mean you had the ability to do whatever you pleased, but that it gave you the ability to make a choice, based on who you already were and what you had learned. It was true, God would manipulate events to his own ends, but we didn't have to like them or go along with them. We simply did what we felt was right, and to us, who had been created to be nothing but mindless servants, that was still a choice.

So Michael and I parted friends, and

with my new understanding of things, I began to actively live among humans, no longer showing my residual gifts from Heaven. I lived completely as a human, fighting against the darkness and the threats in secret. Humanity began to lose its view into the mystical nature, so my job became easier and harder at the same time.

As humans became more logical and science based, I learned I would have to constantly be on the move, lest anyone start to question the oddities surrounding me. I fell in love and married multiple times, as I would guess anyone who lived that long would. It always ended badly, and because of that, I tried to keep myself a loner, living among humans, but maintaining my distance.

You've already heard what happened to one of my wives in France. It was there that I met Loki. He approached me, and asked for my help dealing with some evil witches. They had gotten a hold of one of the Terrarum Exstinctor stones, and were using it as a catalyst in spells, to devastating effect. Loki convinced me that the stones were dangerous, and after studying the history of them, I found this to be true. They were left over relics from the dark days, and when united, they had the power to destroy all life in the realm. There was no information on who had created them, but as I was still in good standing with both

Heaven and Lucifer, I was able to piece together enough information to learn how to locate and destroy them.

That's what I've been doing for the last three hundred years, tracking down the stones in an effort to dispose of them. Information on the location of another stone would come to me every so often, and Loki would show up to help me track them down. During the times in between, Loki would go off to live his own life, and I would continue protecting people, destroying monsters, vampires, witches, werewolves, and all the other creatures that posed a threat.

In recent years, I came to America. Loki came with me, and has spent most of his time by my side. I've always assumed it was because he wanted to spend more time looking for the stones, but I started to realize he just likes being around. As an imp, he doesn't really belong to the realm, but like me, he's taken it for his home. I think in a lot of ways, he just got lonely out there by himself, constantly seeing and fighting things others couldn't see. Honestly, I've been glad for the company. He's got a good heart, and keeps things from ever getting too serious.

A while back, we realized quite a few people were starting to see things humans hadn't seen in quite some time. It was like the veil was being peeled back again. At first I thought maybe it correlated to the fact that less people were believing in religion and God, but I'm starting to wonder if it isn't something else. There's something going on, a string connecting all these dots, but I've never been able to put my finger on it. Maybe it's the beginning of the end times, maybe it's just humanity regaining their old abilities. I don't know.

But, with all this happening, Loki and I decided the best way to help out would be to start up, I guess you'd call it a detective agency. We deal with the things that go bump in the night, the evils that dare not speak their names, spells gone wrong. You'd be surprised how many of those there are.

More than anything though, we do it because we don't want to see any harm done to this place. It's our home now, our world. We've done all we can to protect it, even before we knew each other, and it's what we want to do. We've fought in World Wars, we've found monsters that could swallow the world, and now we have to stop the end of human life. This is just what we do.

The Book of Daniel

15

In which our heroes gear up, another old friend joins the fight, and Danny is reunited with a long-lost love.

"I don't know how much of this helps, if any at all," Danny said. "I just thought you deserved to know what you've been forced into. And I'm really sorry for that. You shouldn't have to deal with all this."

"No," Liz shook her head. "I'm kind of glad I am. It's weird. My whole life, all I've ever wanted is the truth. About anything. I used to drive people crazy, constantly questioning, digging deeper than I should. And now this. Well, it doesn't get any more true than this, does it?"

"Questioning, huh? Yeah, you'll fit right in," Danny said. He gave her a smile. He was relieved that she was accepting all this so easily.

"There's still a lot I don't know, stuff I don't understand," she said. "I guess that's something that comes with time though, right?"

"It does. The longer you're in this world, the more you start to understand. You'd be amazed at how much I still don't know," he told her. "There's a million answers to questions I haven't even asked waiting out there."

"It's nice to know I'm not alone in that," she told him. She gave him a smile, and Danny felt a warmth in his body and wished it away. "I can't ever go back to the way things were, can I?" she asked.

"You could," he said. "Or, you could try. But I have a feeling that you wouldn't be happy with that."

"No, I wouldn't. I still feel like I have a million questions."

"So ask one," he said with a laugh. "I guess we've got time for a little more."

"Gabriel has children," she said.

"Ah, that," Danny rubbed the back of his neck, trying to think of how to answer. "I'm not really sure how to explain. He's the only one I know of that does."

"So, you..."

"I've been married quite a few times, but as far as I know, I don't have any children."

"What about the other angels? You said there were five that stepped down."

Danny stared at the wall opposite them, a dark look growing on his face.

"I don't know about them. We haven't seen them for a very long time. The last time we did... well, it was a bad day," he told her.

Loki decided to pop into the room just then, and Danny was grateful for it. As much as he wanted Liz to understand everything, there were some things he just wasn't ready to tell her about yet.

"How's the magical mystery tour?" the imp asked.

"Eye-opening and confusing," Liz told him.

"Yeah, welcome to my world," Loki laughed.

"Has he been talking about me the whole time? He does that a lot."

"Oh, yeah, I don't know anything about angels, but I've heard all about you."

Loki smiled at her, a charming and mischievous smile. "I'm a bona fide hero. Killed the Loch Ness monster, you know? Course, it wasn't the real one, and I did it by accident, but, hey, never let the truth get in the way of a good story."

"What's up, Loki?" Danny asked.

"They're ready for us," he responded.

Danny and Liz followed him out, back into the warehouse. They could hear Gabriel and Michael talking from a distance.

"Did you see some of the women?" Loki asked. "I think they're just my type."

"They're the children of an angel. I think they'd rip you in half," Danny told him.

"Yeah, but I'd enjoy every minute of it."

They came to a stop behind Gabriel and Michael. Gabriel turned around, his face deadly serious.

"I've done everything I can," he said. "It's not much, but it should be enough to get you inside to stop the spell."

"I notice you're not saying whether we'll make it back out," Danny said.

Gabriel shrugged. "I've done what I can," he said.

He motioned towards the table. Danny stepped up to it and inventoried what they had. There were a couple of daggers, two swords that had seen better days, and a hatchet. Sitting next to the hatchet was a large brown box.

"I know how it looks," Gabriel said. Danny merely waved his explanation away.

"We've fought with less," he said.

"You won't be alone," Gabriel told him. "I'm going with you, as is when of my men."

"One of your sons?" Loki asked.

"Not quite."

"You don't have to do that, Gabe," Danny told him. "It's not your fight."

"Yes it is, amigo. Michael explained it to me. There's no way I'm letting those punks pull this off. I've spent far too long here to lose it to wannabe, know-it-all, third wave angels." He gave them a calm smile. "Besides, I haven't had any real excitement in years."

"I thought you hated excitement?" Danny asked.

"Sometimes you need a little something to make paradise seem that much brighter."

Liz pointed to the box.

"What's in there?"

"Ah, that is my secret weapon," Gabe told them. He opened the box to reveal a pile of loose bullets. "Angel killers."

Liz picked one up and looked at it closely.

".45's?" she asked.

Gabe nodded his head in appreciation. "They are. Do you know how?" he asked, pulling an empty clip from his pocket. Liz took the clip and quickly loaded it.

"Nice," Loki said under his breath.

"How are they angel killers?" Danny asked.

"When I left Heaven, I managed to sneak a few things out. One of them was my old sword,"

Gabe answered.

Michael gave Gabe an unhappy look.

"That was not appropriate," Michael said.

"Probably not, but it's going to come in handy now."

"Gabe, you didn't," Danny said.

"Yep," Gabe responded.

Liz and Loki both looked confused, so Liz asked, "What am I missing?"

"He melted down his flaming sword and turned it into bullets," Danny told her.

"If you want to kill an angel, you must use the weapon of an angel. I just updated it a bit," Gabe said, beaming with pride.

Danny patted him on the shoulder. "Nicely done," he said.

"You got a gun?" Liz asked.

Gabe reached underneath the table and pulled out two silver .45's. He handed them to Liz.

Liz took the weapons and sat one on the table. With the other one, she popped the clip into place, pulled the slide to load the chamber, then held her eye up to check the sights. Danny and Loki were astonished.

"Have I mentioned how much I really like her?" the imp asked.

"You know how to use those?" Danny asked. "More specifically, are you any good with them?"

"I work in the ER," she said. "You're damn right I know how to use one. And I"m deadly with it."

"Guess we know who's got those," Loki said. He made his way to the table, and after carefully looking at the weapons, chose the hatchet. He tucked it away in his belt.

"The bullets are the only things I am definitely sure will be fatal," Michael told the group.

"The others probably won't kill, but they've all been heavily enchanted," Gabe said. "It won't put an angel down, but they'll know they've been in a fight."

"Guess that will have to be good enough," Danny said. He started to pick up one of the swords, but Gabe stopped him.

"I actually have something special for you," he told Danny. "Should be here any... there he is now."

Making his way through the warehouse was a lanky man wearing an overly loud Hawaiian shirt and ripped khaki shorts. His shoulder length dirty blond hair bounced as he walked. In one hand, he carried something wrapped in a dark silk.

"Raphael?" Danny asked in amazement.

"What's going on, D?" the man asked as he reached the group.

"Raphael?" Liz asked. "So he's either a ninja turtle or another angel."

"Oh, I'm neither, little lady," he said. "I'm a surfer."

"Uh huh," she said with some skepticism.

"Raph used to be an angel," Danny told her.

"Stepped down?"

"Nope," Raph said proudly. "I just gave it up."

"You gave it up?" Liz repeated.

"Yeah."

"How does someone just 'give up' being an

angel?" she asked.

"I just stopped going," he told her.

Liz looked at Danny. "I don't understand that," she said.

"It's just like any other job," Raph explained. "I didn't like it anymore, so I stopped going to work."

"And now you're a surfer?"

"Pretty much," he said.

"Well, that doesn't really comfort me any," Liz said.

"What are you doing here anyway?" Danny asked him.

"Best waves away from the islands," Raph told him. "Stopped in to grab a drink, and Gabe told me what was going down, so I thought I'd help." He raised the package he held in his hand. "Plus, I brought a little something."

Raphael handed the package to Danny. He opened it, and his jaw fell open in shock.

"What is it?" Loki asked.

"It's a sword," Danny told him. "It's just like the one I used to have."

"Actually, it is the one you used to have," Gabe told him. "I was doing business with a Russian a few years back. This had happened to come into his possession, and he was wanting to trade it. I thought I might hold on to it until I saw you again."

Danny picked up the sword and held it gently, looking over the polished steel, checking the grip, feeling its comforting weight. From beside him, Loki appreciated the weapon.

"Katana?" the imp asked.

"Yeah, one of the finest pieces of Japanese steel ever made, or so I'm told," Danny said.

"Can I?" Loki asked.

Danny handed the sword to him. The blade stood almost as tall as him. He swung it a few times, nodded and handed it back to Danny.

"So what's the big deal about this thing?" Liz asked.

"Yeah, I've always wondered that myself," Loki said. "I think I've only seen you use it once."

Danny looked at the sword a moment longer, before setting it gingerly down on the table.

"It was given to me by an old monk. They were having some problems with a group of demons trying to overrun the monastery, so they had called me in," Danny told them. "As it turned out, the demons were actually lead by one of the Fallen angels. I wasn't sure if I could kill a former angel with the weapons I had."

"I've been meaning to ask about that," Liz said. "I"m guessing from everything we've been doing here, it takes something special to kill an angel."

It was Michael who answered her.

"An angel may only be killed by a flaming sword, the weapon of an angel, or by a weapon that has been touched by God," the angel told her.

"Right," Danny nodded. "We were never sure how that applied to former angels though. So the monk gave me this. Told me it had been touched by the hand of God Himself. I don't know that I really believe him, but I gotta say, it's been probably the best sword I've ever owned. It can cut through anything, never loses its shine, and always seems to hit its mark."

"Let's just hope it's enough," Loki said.

Danny agreed, privately hoping they make it through all this without really having to find out.

"So we have a team, we have weapons, do we have a location?" Gabe asked.

"Um, no, not as such," Loki told him.

"That makes the job a bit more difficult."

"I've been thinking about that," Danny said. "They could do the spell just about anywhere, but I don't think they would have gone far from Austin."

"With Augustyne's powers, they could have gone anywhere in existence, Daniel," Michael told him.

"I know, but I just have a hunch," Danny said. He turned to Liz. "Jason's doing the spell with Augustyne. Any ideas on where he'd go for something like this?"

Liz pursed her lips and thought it over. She started to shake her head, then stopped and rethought.

"Jason always talked about places that he felt were centers of occult and mystic power," she told them. "One place he'd actually mentioned recently. The Alamo."

"The theater?" Loki asked.

Danny slapped his forehead.

"No, the actual historical site. Of course!" he said. "When we were at his house, he had some papers he was looking over. One of them was the blueprints for the Alamo. I thought it looked familiar, but couldn't place it at the time.'"

"Jason was really on a kick about that lately," Liz said. "Something about old Nazi paperwork and blood magic."

Gabe audibly scoffed at this. Michael shook their head in a stern manner.

"There's no such thing as blood magic. It has no true power," they said.

"What is it?" Liz asked.

"Some people believe spilled blood has a power to it," Loki told her. "They think that places where a massacre occurred, such as the site of a serial killing or a battle, can be marked by this blood and amplify magic and spells that are used there."

Everyone turned to stare at Loki.

"What?" he asked. "I read books occasional-ly."

"I think Liz is right. Jason had the plans for the place. Whether the blood magic would help or not, I think it's the place. And it's only an hour or so south of Austin," Danny said.

"Then we go and check it out," Gabe said.

"Might as well start somewhere," Loki agreed.

"Michael?" Danny asked.

"Yes, we will go there first," Michael said. The angel held out both hands. Everyone formed a circle, joining their hands together.

Michael took them back to Texas.

16

In which the good guys face the bad guys.

They appeared as if out of nowhere, in an abandoned building just down the street. Danny was on the move before Liz had even realized where they were. Traveling with an angel would take some time for her to get used to.

Danny held up his hand, having the others stay back. He crept to the nearest door and poked his head out. After what seemed like a long minute, he came back in and shut the door.

"This is definitely the right place," he told them.

"How many?" Gabe asked.

"Four out front, two on the roof," Danny said. "I'm guessing more inside. Not as bad as I'd thought, but not good either."

"I believe many angels are waiting to see the outcome of this," Michael said. "Few would openly risk something so bold for fear of being caught."

"That sounds like us," Raph laughed.

"Raph and I can take the angels on the street," Gabe said. He turned to Liz. "Can you hit the two on the roof?"

"If I can get close enough," she said. "You think you can take four angels?"

"I was the keeper of Heaven's armory," Gabe

said, giving her his million dollar smile. "There is no one I can't best in combat."

"And what about you?" she asked Raphael.

"Oh, I should be fine. I was in charge of cleanliness," he answered. She looked at the ripped and dirty shorts, the unkempt hair, and misbuttoned shirt.

"Yeah, I can see that," she said.

"It's next to godliness, you know," he called after her, as she made her way to the door. Danny stopped her.

"I have an idea," he said.

Danny reached into his shirt and pulled the amulet out. He let his fingers run across it one last time, then took it off and placed it around Liz's neck.

"It's a protection charm," he told her. "It makes the wearer invisible to enemies. It won't hide me from angels though. Something about being related, I guess."

She held the amulet in her hands.

"Thank you," she said. She hesitated for a moment, then leaned up and kissed him on the cheek. "For luck," she told him.

"I could use some luck too," Loki said. She smiled and patted him on the head instead.

Gabe and Raph stood behind Liz, each holding one of the old swords.

"The three of us will go first. Once we've got them distracted and Liz has taken out the guards up top, you make a run for it," Gabe told them.

The three exited the building. Danny left the door open just enough for him to watch their progress. They were within twenty feet of the Alamo when the guards noticed them. They called out, and Gabe and Raph put their hands in the air, still walking, approaching the guards. They couldn't even see Liz, but she had stopped and taken up a position, ready to shoot.

Loki pulled the hatchet from his belt. He gave Michael a look.

"Didn't see you pick up a weapon," he said.

"I have my own, little one."

From within their trench coat, Michael pulled out a shining sword. Once free of the coat, the blade immediately burst into flames. It made Michael look quite intimidating.

"Yeah, that definitely works," Loki said.

The guards had stopped Gabe and Raph and were talking to them. With a suddenness that shocked even Danny, Gabe brought down the hand holding the sword, and hacked into the arm of the angel nearest him. He spun quickly to block a blow coming from another angel, pulling out his dagger and using it to stab the first.

At the same time, Raph sent a kick into the angel nearest him and jabbed his sword into the neck of the other. Before he was finished with that maneuver, Danny heard gunshots, three in total. He saw both angels from the rooftop drop to the ground, not moving.

Danny threw the door open, running full speed, Michael a step behind, easily keeping pace, Loki trailing back, struggling to keep up.

"Liz!" Danny yelled out. "Shoot them!"

He saw Liz turn just as they were approaching her. She had a .45 in each hand, and this time wasted no bullets, firing four times, hitting all four angels.

"Nice shooting," Danny said.

"You should have let us have them. Saved the bullets for inside," Gabe said.

"Don't worry, I'm sure there will plenty of those third wavers to fight inside," Danny told him. He could feel it, as he knew his siblings could, the adrenaline rising, the blood pumping quickly. The heat of the battle was taking over.

Danny lead the way inside the outer wall, into the courtyard of the Alamo. Seven angels stood waiting for them, all with flaming swords in hand. Danny saw Geonosius standing towards the back of the group.

"The big one's mine," Loki said, charging headlong into the group of angels. As he ran, each angel took a swipe at him, each missing completely. This gave Danny and the others the opening they needed.

They waded in, Danny making sure to keep Liz close. It was clear that Danny and his group were the superior fighters, as the angels were falling back a step at a time, trying to parry the heavy blows landing on them.

"Should I fire?" Liz shouted, as Danny blocked a counter attack.

"No, save them," Danny responded. He rammed his blade into the chest of the angel he was fighting with. He was surprised when the angel dropped to his knees. The light of life left their eyes, and they fell over, dead.

"Damn," he said. "Guess the monk was right. My sword really was touched by God."

He turned to find another opponent, his eyes catching Michael, flaming sword locked up with another.

"Go, Daniel!" Michael shouted to him. "Stop the spell!"

Danny grabbed Liz and headed into the old fort, running past Loki as he buried his hatchet into the knees of Geonosius. The large angel fell over, and Loki was on him in an instant, hacking away at the angel's head.

Danny and Liz entered the fort quietly. From somewhere towards the back, they head voices. Danny placed a finger over his lips and lead Liz back towards the voices.

In the center of a large room, a fire burned. Encircling it were the stones. Beside the fire, Augustyne sat, their legs crossed, head held high, repeating the spell. Every so often, they would throw a mixture of powder and roots into the flames. Just outside of the stones, several sacred circles were set up, making sure no angels could get through to Augustyne.

Laying next to the angel was Jason. He was tied up, hands and feet bound, a gag in his mouth. His eyes bulged with each toss of materials. He was bleeding badly from cuts on his torso. Danny understood at once. In order for the spell to be specific on destroying only humans, Augustyne needed human blood to add to the spell. It seemed they had failed to mention that part to Jason.

Jason's eyebrows shot up in surprise. Danny realized they were visible, so he pulled Liz back into the other room.

"Could he see me?" she whispered.

"I think so. He must not truly be an enemy," he told her.

"How is that possible?"

"Maybe he still has good feelings for you," Danny said. "That's not what's worrying me right now. Augustyne has sacred circles placed around the room. I can't get to them with those circles in place."

"I'll take care of those," Liz said.

"Just, whatever you do, make sure Augustyne doesn't know you're there," Danny told her. "We have to hurry. If they're adding human blood, that means they've almost reached the end."

"That is correct, Daniel," Augustyne called from the other room. Danny rolled his eyes in frustration. "Yes, I can hear you. I am not so wrapped up in what I am doing that I cannot hear you trying to whisper. Come in here so I can see you."

Danny stepped around the corner. Augustyne smiled at him, then nodded towards Danny's sword. Danny put it down on the ground.

"Welcome to the glorious end of all humanity, Daniel," the angel told him. "Where is your friend?"

"I don't know what you mean."

"Do not try and fool me. I heard you speaking with someone. Where are they?"

"It's just me, Augustyne," Danny said. He looked at Jason. "Why don't you let the guy go?"

A scowl crossed Augustyne's face. "Tell me

who you were talking to," they demanded.

Danny laughed. "Do you see anyone else here? Maybe I was just talking to God."

It was Augustyne's turn to laugh.

"By now, you know as well as I that God has been gone for quite some time," Augustyne told him. Danny simply smiled. He could see Liz out of the corner of his eye. She was creeping into the room, making sure the angel couldn't see her. When she was sure he couldn't, she leaned down and put her hand on the sword, but stopped, trying to figure out how to move it without Augustyne seeing. Danny was doing his best not to look at her.

"If you want, you can always come over here and check for yourself," Danny told the angel. He was doing the best he could to buy Liz time.

"I am sorry, but I am not as foolish as you, Daniel, constantly jumping into situations without looking," Augustyne told him. Instead of picking the sword up, Liz began to slowly move it towards one of the circles, moving it slowly, minute distances at a time. "You know, if you would have only paid attention, you would not have ended up in this situation."

"I'm sure you're right," Danny said. "Neither would poor Jason."

"Yes, the boy was quite foolish to trust me, but putting his faith in an angel will pay off for all of us," Augustyne said. They looked down at Jason, and noticed the man staring in wide-eyed anxiety. The angel looked up, trying to see what Jason saw. "What are you looking at, boy?"

Danny needed to keep their attention distracted, needed to keep them talking.

"So, what, you just made a deal that he'd survive while every other human died? Then you took it all back?" Danny asked.

Distracted, Augustyne responded, "I told him I would make him one of us. What do you see?" They grabbed Jason's face, still staring out at nothingness.

"You're getting paranoid," Danny told them. "You've managed to fool all of Heaven and Earth. You should be happy you made it this far."

Liz had gotten the tip of the sword to the edge of the circles. She was hoping she could pull this off. She began very lightly rubbing the sword tip against the edge, trying to scrape it off quietly, breaking the circle.

"Your friend is here," Augustyne said. They picked up their flaming sword. "I cannot see them for some reason. Very tricky, Daniel. But it will not save you. You have lost and humanity is dead."

Augustyne reached out as far as they could, the edge of their sword reaching just past the circles and began swinging. Liz stayed as low as she could to the ground, the blade passing just inches from her head. She pushed the sword harder, grinding away.

"Where are you?" Augustyne shouted. "Where are you?"

Liz managed to rub off the edge of the circle just as Augustyne began to bring the flaming sword down directly on her position.

"Liz!"

Liz rolled and threw the sword to Danny,

who caught it on the run, his feet already inside the circle. Augustyne had only a second to recover before Danny was on them, their blades clashing and parting, clashing and parting. Augustyne spun them around, lowered their shoulder and knocked Danny into the fire. Danny quickly rolled out of it, and narrowly missed Augustyne's blade chopping down. He jumped up quickly, and locked up with the angel again.

Augustyne leaned in and said to Danny, "You are a fool. You may be a good fighter, but I am an angel." With that, Augustyne grabbed Danny.

Danny felt the world spin and knew they were porting. He looked around to see they were now floating in nothingness, drifting through the space between realms.

"Enjoy eternity," Augustyne told him. The angel pushed Danny away hard. Danny had only a split second to react, just barely grabbing the edge of Augustyne's jacket as they ported back.

Danny fell on his back with a crash. He looked up to see Augustyne standing over him, flaming sword held over their head, ready to bring down the killing blow. Just as they started the downward motion, Danny saw a blade on fire poke its way through Augustyne's chest. The angel looked down at it, a look of surprise and disappointment crossing their face. They turned to face their attacker.

Michael stood behind Augustyne, the older angel's face cold and emotionless.

"But you were my partner," Augustyne said.

"You were not a good partner," Michael responded. Augustyne fell to the ground dead.

Danny dropped his head and lay on the floor panting. Loki made his way from the door to Danny's side.

"So, don't go dying on me or anything, but Mikey over there just made a quip," Loki said. "It's a day of miracles."

"I'm fine, Loki," Danny said. "Just exhausted."

"Works not over yet, boss. We've still got the stones to destroy."

Danny sighed as he got to his feet.

"Michael, we need the supplies to destroy the stones. Do you know what to get?" he asked.

"The imp has informed me," the angel said. With the blink of an eye they were gone.

"How are the others?" Danny asked.

"Oh, they're fine. The killjoy kept taking out all the angels while we had them distracted. I could've taken that big guy, boss, I swear," Loki said. He lead Danny over to the wall to lean on for more support.

"I know you could have." Danny looked over at Liz. "You know, you could have shot him at just about any time there," he said.

"You told me not to be seen, no matter what," she answered. "Besides, I thought maybe you wanted to be the one to take him out."

"I did, but the moment he started kicking my ass, I wouldn't have minded some help."

"What are we going to do with him?" Loki asked, looking towards Jason.

"Guess we should probably untie him."

Loki used the edge of his hatchet to cut through the ropes. Jason rubbed his wrists once he was free, then stood up to face Liz.

"Liz, baby, I-"

He didn't get to finish his sentence. Liz kicked him hard in the crotch. He doubled over, letting out a moan. She took the opening to uppercut him, sending him falling over onto his back. She leaned over him and smiled sweetly.

"Don't ever touch me again," she said happily. Jason crawled backwards away from her, out the door, and disappeared into the night.

The Book of Daniel

Interlude
The Alamo

The two figures stood in darkness, watching the events unfold. She had wanted to get involved, but he held her back. They knew it was all said and done when they saw the last of the flaming swords disappear.

"We're not supposed to intervene, unless it appears things ain't going the way they need to. It don't look like that, though. Looks like the good guys win again," Bob told her. "I'd damn sure like to get my hands on one of those angels, but we're simply here to watch. To make sure these fools don't go and screw up everything."

Jezebel nodded. She didn't quite know all the details, but she somehow knew they had won tonight.

"What were they doing in there?" she asked him.

"Playing around with things they shouldn't be," he answered. "Thinking they could go about destroying that which God had put forth. But that ain't their place."

"It's our masters'."

"That's right, darlin'. From darkness to light, back to darkness. It ain't for the angels to decide. It's for those that were here first. We was just here to make sure they didn't go and kill off humans. That right belongs to our masters" Bob said. He leaned down and kissed her.

"It's time to go, baby," she told him. "We've got work to do in other places. In Europe, in the old world."

Bob looked at her, startled.

"The voices," she said. "I can hear them. They're calling to me."

Bob smiled. "Soon enough, they'll be calling out to all of us, all us creatures of the night."

They kissed again. The two were just turning to leave, when they saw a lone figure leaving the fort, bent over as if in pain, looking back over his shoulder.

"Guess there wouldn't be nothing wrong with a bite to eat first, would there?" Jezebel asked.

"Darlin', you are insatiable."

The two vampires followed the figure, excited for their next meal.

17

In which Danny and Loki finally finish their mission, old enemies enact revenge, and a new mission begins.

Michael reappeared, carrying a bag full of supplies. They handed the bag to Danny. Danny and Loki gathered the stones together. The two stood before the fire, and stopped to look at each other.

"Well, it's been a long run," Danny said.

"Yep. Glad to have it done?"

"I am. You?"

"Of course. Don't think I'm going to miss this at all."

"You're leaving after this?"

C'mon, boss. Do you really think there's anywhere I'd rather be? Austin's my place."

"Okay then, let's do it."

Together, the two threw the stones into the fire. Danny opened the bag, and began adding the items to the fire, speaking an incantation with each one. Before he added the last, he turned back to Loki.

"You want to do the honors?" he asked.

"You know I don't speak Latin."

Danny laughed and added the last ingredient. The flames shot up, dark blue and cold, before settling back down to a normal burn.

"That's it?" Liz asked.

"We have to wait for them to finish melting and say another incantation, but, yeah, that's it," Danny said. He turned, his back to the fire, and smiled.

"Well, that was anti-climactic. Now what?" Liz asked.

"We go back to our lives," Danny told her.

"I'm just supposed to go back to the ER like nothing happened? I'm not sure I can do that."

"I guess maybe we could still hang out," Danny said. He smiled back at her, a deep, caring smile. He was already thinking that he would like to spend a lot more time with her.

"Guess we go back to just handling cases," Loki said.

Danny looked at Michael. The angel looked out of place, like a lost little boy.

"Actually," Danny said, "I was thinking maybe we should take on another mission. Maybe it's time we went out and found God."

Michael looked at him, with an expression that wasn't quite happiness. Danny understood anyway.

"You know, I've heard people say that, but never mean it literally," Liz said.

"Yeah, well, I guess-"

Danny didn't get to finish his thought. The flames behind him shot up, all the way to the ceiling. Loki was knocked back by the force of it.

"The amulet," Danny yelled out. There was no time to react.

Three pairs of hands, dark, scaly, clawed hands, reached out of the flames. They grabbed Danny tightly and pulled him in. Loki made a desperate scramble to grab hold of Danny, but didn't make it. In the blink of an eye, Danny was gone.

The three stood in stunned silence.

"What just happened?" Liz asked, her face a mask of shock.

Loki stood up. The flames were still tall, but they were gradually shrinking. The imp stood looking into the fire for a moment, before digging into his pocket. He pulled out the stub of a cigar.

"Guess we do have another mission after all," he said. He bent down and used the flames to light the cigar.

"Looks like we've got to rescue Danny from Hell."

**To Be Continued in
The Book of Daniel:
Sins of the Past**

The Book of Daniel

Acknowledgements

I want to give thanks to my partner Tabitha for convincing me to keep writing. You have no idea how much your support means.

Also, a huge thanks goes out to the city of Austin, TX. From the moment I set foot in the city, and all through the short time I lived there, I felt extremely alive and inspired. You will always hold a piece of my heart and be my home away from home, Austin.